RAVEN BLOOD

THE RED MASQUES SERIES - BOOK 1

M. SINCLAIR

Formatted By Kassie Morse

The Union of Love & Madness

CONTENTS

DESCRIPTION

No one in our family had come from an easy life. From foster care to forming the Ravens at our small Boston college, the concept of danger had never been one we turned away from. Instead, we took it upon ourselves to serve as the lawless justice system on campus to stop unnecessary deaths from the distribution of laced drug products.

Why? Because of her. Because her death could have been stopped. That was why we formed the Ravens.

So what has changed? My boys have always been protective but now I felt as though there was a secret standing between us. As we begin to receive tips about the Letters, questions start to plague my mind. What have the boys been hiding from me? Why is my sister, Lucida, never around anymore? Why do dead ravens continue to show up in my home? Why can't I stop thinking about fire?

You have to understand, nothing has ever been simple for us. You try living in a house with all boys. Boys that you...

well, I'm not positive how I feel about them. Something has always been different about us. I can feel it. So, my biggest question -- what is it?

The Ravens. Ready yourself for chaos, love, and gore. Nothing is simple or easy for Vegas.

Paranormal Urban Fantasy RH Our badass characters swear a lot. As well, please be advised that the book contains darker themes including assault, PTSD, and violence. Additionally, sexual themes are suitable for mature audiences +18.

VEGAS

"**I** didn't know," the man whimpered in a small pathetic voice. "I was doing what I was told."

"You didn't know your fucking product was laced?" Grover spoke in a low, frustrated voice. His hand was firmly fixed against the man's throat like an iron manacle.

"Product quality isn't my job," he responded in a strangled voice.

With mild disgust written across his features, Grover dropped the man to his feet and stepped back. I could see the sweat that had built upon the man's forehead and the mild tremor that worked its way through his spine. I didn't exactly look *down* on his palpable fear because Grover could be somewhat intimidating. However, Laurence had placed himself in this situation, and therefore, had no one to blame but himself. What type of dealer doesn't confirm their product quality?

A very inexperienced one.

"Laurence," I spoke in a smooth voice from the darkness of the alley. "You're going to accompany Blue and show him every single person you sold to tonight. You're going to explain the obvious lapse in judgment you suffered and return their money."

"But my contact-"

"I don't care how this affects you," I responded mildly. "Just go."

Blue's smile was utterly deceptive. His dimples made him appear harmless, but the wicked glint in his baby blues told another story. Out of all the Ravens, Blue had the darkest streak. He pressed a kiss to my temple and grasped Laurence by the back of his hoodie. The two of them made their way from the alley.

"Do you want me to drive you home? Blue has this covered." Grover's voice was much smoother now. Less angry. His voice had a natural charm to it that lured others in. I smiled at him and took a moment to appreciate his sweet gesture. I knew he wanted to go back inside though. Grover loved being the center of attention. He had been that way since high school.

Honestly, it wasn't challenging to be the center of attention when you looked like him.

"I'm going to call Rocket," I murmured while pretending to send a text. "Get your ass back to drinking."

Grover chuckled, squeezed my shoulder, and walked back through the alley entrance. As he opened the back door, I heard the loud music emitting from the bar. The smell of alcohol permeated the chilled autumn air. I was relatively surprised he didn't stay and wait for me to get picked up.

I laughed softly as realization dawned on me. He knew. He knew I was taking this time to myself. My sneakers scuffed lightly against the gravel as my mind wandered. These long peaceful walks were really the only quiet I had throughout the day. The large Victorian house the nine of us occupied was always filled with noise and destructive pranks. I didn't mind the chaos, but these 3 a.m. walks were essential to maintaining my sanity.

As the unspoken leader of the Ravens, my responsibilities were numerous and time-consuming. From assuring all members maintained their school status too late-night quality confrontations, there was very little room in my life for relaxation. As the university grew in size, increasing rapidly in just the past three years, so did our responsibilities. We served as the unofficial justice system for the baser population of the school. We monitored illegal activity and stepped in when needed. For instance, we hopped in if drugs were being laced with unknown substances and clients were purchasing these products unaware of the possible danger. I liked to think of us as a Robin Hood group. Lawless justice and all that shit.

On some level, even in high school, we understood that stopping drug sales was an impossible feat. *Hell* – most of us had used them at some point. However, avoiding unnecessary deaths was something we took pride in. Mostly because of her. She was the reason that I was up at 3 a.m. each morning. Her death had changed everything for me. For the ten of us.

The Ravens were well known throughout campus and well-liked for the most part. Unless you were a drug dealer. Then we were probably pretty frightening. To keep tabs on that specific sector of the populace, we had Rocket act as an intermediate between some of the larger drug groups and clients. He often took the product given to him and tested its quality in his lab.

Yeah. A lab. You heard me. My boy Rocket had a creepy basement lab that I avoided at all costs.

While each member of our group was essential to our

purpose, they were not chosen. No, it had always been the ten of us. Our strength was not only showcased in our emotional bond but our individual skill sets. I liked to think that was in part due to me. I always tried to encourage them to pursue interests outside of the Ravens. The response back usually consisted of an eye roll, scoff, and chuckle. *Apparently,* no one had an interest in expanding outside of our little family.

I loved our family, even if we were a tad unusual. When you place ten forgotten foster kids together at a young age, they usually stick together. It had always been the boys, Lucida, and myself. I heard the rumors about the ten of us, specifically the boys and me, but found myself bored with their insinuations. Why did I care about their useless and unimportant opinions?

Unfortunately, that didn't stop me from noticing. Noticing what, you ask? Everything. I wanted to believe my unusual perspective made me a better friend. I mean, what's better than a friend that noticed every physical and vocal cue you gave off? Right?

Yeah. Probably not.

I heard, felt, and saw so many different emotions and opinions that my empathetic nature often felt overwhelming. Instead of dealing with the chaos in my head, I focused on others. Specifically, Lucida and my boys. We were an isolated bunch.

On the small chance that someone outside of the Ravens was brought over, they were usually met with uncomfortable glances and suspicious questions. Lucida's girlfriend, Miranda, was one of the only exceptions and she lived in Chicago. The boys had made an unofficial rule that outside of Lucida and I, other girls were not allowed on the property.

So you are probably wondering what dating is like for me?

To that, I respond, *what fucking dates?* Trying to do anything with any male outside of our group was a special type of hell. Actually, that didn't even quantify the problem it caused within the house. Could I go on a date? Sure. Would I be followed? Absolutely. Could I bring them home? No fucking way.

So that's fun.

In high school, I had been with one guy. He had been sweet and fun until he wasn't anymore. After losing my virginity to him in an entirely anti-climactic way, literally, he had broken up with me. I had landed myself a bruised ego, and he landed himself a broken rib curtsey of Decimus. Since then, I have managed one or two hookups. Each one of them had avoided me after and not in the *oh Vegas I really did mean to call you back* way. No. This was the type of avoidance were spotting me across the street resulted in an abrupt about-face. If it weren't for the overprotective masculinity hovering around me at all times, I would doubt my ability in bed. As it stood, I had an excellent idea of why they were avoiding me and luckily, it had nothing to do with the bedroom.

As I mentioned before, these 3 a.m. walks were for my sanity.

It was bullshit since I knew, fucking *knew,* that the boys weren't avoiding hookups. Well, the only one I had confirmation on, regarding that, was Grover. Even then, it had only been once. I just can't imagine my boys not dating. They were an exceptionally handsome group of men. Men like them hooked up. Right?

"Vegas," a deep baritone voice called from ahead of me. My eyes shot up from my sneakers to the large Victorian house that loomed ahead. The scent of mint and fresh laundry filled my senses. I smiled.

"Rocket," I teased. I could tell he was upset. I hadn't called for a ride. A ride he was supposed to give me. Then again, when was Rocket not upset? He was such an asshole. Like, all the time. It didn't help that he was a socially inept genius.

"Why are you so fucking stubborn?" He spoke quietly with a soft rumble echoing in his chest. I had felt my phone buzz several times and deduced that he had been the one calling me. Even now, he held the keys to one of our family cars in his left hand.

"Because you love it," I smiled. He was dressed in lounge clothes with an oversized hoodie and joggers. It was so unlike him to wear comfortable clothes that I nearly did a double-take.

I narrowed my eyes at his messy hair as we began trailing up the driveway. Rocket was usually quiet, but tonight he just seemed exhausted. Also, his hair either needed a trim or he had been doing that thing where he runs his hand through his hair a million times. If I had to guess it was both.

"I don't need a haircut," he mumbled quietly. The man noticed everything.

I snickered and lifted a hand to his hair in a playful ruffle. It was a color that women paid thousands for. The sides of his hair were short and dark brown while the top of his head was a mess of wavy blonde and platinum waves. It was a pleasant contrast that was only accented further by his dark brows and angular face. It was the type of look that companies searched the globe for. The man was gorgeous. If it weren't for his inability to talk to literally anyone outside of our group, he would probably be getting laid regularly. I frowned at that thought and tried to ignore the tightness in my chest.

"Who's home?"

Our house was lit up far more than usual for 3 a.m. The Victorian wasn't anything spectacular, but it was home. The structure was long and tall with dark blue siding and a black roof. The porch was a little shaky and the appliances dated, but nothing could compare to the feeling of warmth that accompanied its presence.

Rocket followed me through the front door as I realized the need for such a bright light. Accompanied by the smell of paint, Booker turned to greet us while stepping around the couch that had been shifted to the side. I immediately let out a laugh.

"What?" he asked with amusement as his eyes met mine. His light grey eyes always reminded me of soft velvet. Rocket and Booker shared very similar grey eyes, angular features, and soft structured lips. However, their matching qualities ended there. Rocket was built of lean, defined muscle. Booker was far more bulky and muscular. Although it wasn't fair to compare them because the conclusion was always the same – they were both very handsome.

Our resident artist and musician, Booker, was a shirtless painted mess tonight. He often worked shirtless, but as of late, it had grown more distracting. Can you blame a girl? You try to stay focused with a muscular tan god walking around in only a pair of paint-splattered jeans. I turned my attention back to the paint and not his impressive set of abs. The bright purple he had been using had taken residence in his shoulder-length hair. Despite his attempt to pull it back, the dark blonde pieces were plastered against his golden skin.

"Booker, you do realize you're covered in paint?" I asked

curiously. Our second-hand furniture was all pushed to the left side of the narrow room. Rocket had his laptop set up with a beer nearby. The two of them were rarely away from one another. Both boys enjoyed the solitude of silence. I think it allowed both of them to think more clearly. So it didn't surprise me they were using this opportunity of an empty house.

Booker looked down at me and chuckled. "I guess I am, how perceptive of you, Vegas."

I rolled my eyes at Rocket's chuckle. Booker turned back to his lavender wall and sighed with disappointment. I moved to stand next to him while ignoring the heat his body gave off.

"Not the base color you wanted?"

"I want this mural to be perfect," he groaned softly with frustration. "I just can't find the shade of purple that matches what I am seeing."

"Why don't you make the color?"

Silence.

"Brilliant as always," Rocket sighed from his laptop. Confused, I looked up at Booker, and his bright eyes were sparkling in anticipation. There was something else there as well, something I tried to ignore. It wouldn't do me any good to think like that.

"This is why," he grinned again and pressed a kiss to my cheek.

I didn't ask the why but assumed it was something along the lines of "*this is why you're my best friend and the most exceptional woman on this damn planet.*"

At least that was my hope.

"All right, boys," I sighed. "I have exhausted my genius for the evening."

"Night," both of them called out.

My feet scuffed the varnished wood stairs that Grover had completed this previous summer. I dragged myself up the steps with exhausted movements and muttered groans. I heard the front door open behind me and brace for impact.

"Beautiful!" Blue called out in an incredible raspy voice. My feet went from being planted on the ground at the top of the steps to being lifted off in one swift movement.

"So tired," I muttered. There was no point in fighting him. He was a hugger and cuddler. I let him carry me along the dark hallway to my designated bedroom. My lips were pressed against his neck as I breathed in the scent of cinnamon. It reminded me of Fireball whiskey.

"Hey you ginger bum," another familiar voice mumbled. From my room, I might add. Blue put me down as my narrowed sleepy eyes focused on the person occupying my bed. Fucking Decimus.

If Blue was a bright flame, Decimus was absolute darkness. Both were intimidatingly tall and muscular. Both smelled like different alcohol – one cinnamon whiskey and the other tequila. One was a sweetheart. The other was a total asshole. One hid his dark streak. The other embraced it. Both were codependent needy shits, though. They were also my cuddle buddies, and I loved them for it.

I knew. I knew what it sounded like. Honest to god, though, I had never kissed either of them. It wasn't from a lack of attraction. Decimus, or Deci, had beautiful ebony hair that he wore combed back. His features were dark and masculine, paired with beautiful ivory skin and honey-colored eyes. Deci had come from a massive Greek family before foster care and cursed in fluent Greek when angry. It prevented any of us from being too offended by his terrible temper.

"Don't smoke in my room," I growled softly. My room

was larger than most in the house. Without a conversation, the boys had placed me in the large master bedroom. The tradeoff? I often came home to one or two of them wanting to cuddle. I never locked my room because I honestly didn't mind one bit. Human affection and love was something we grew up with very little of. At least, before we had been placed together.

"Fine," he growled back. My lip twitched at his annoyed tone. I authentically loved arguing with Decimus because it always seemed to have this heated and sexy undertone to it. Then again, it was entirely possible that I imagined that.

My room was dark as I stumbled around to sort out my sleeping clothes for the night. I was confident the shirt I found wasn't mine originally. The instant I smelled vanilla and bamboo body wash, I knew it was Grover's shirt. The bastard always used my fucking body wash.

I sighed and wondered - nix that - worried just how late he would be out.

Without much thought, I pulled off my half top and bra. My back was to the boys, but they had seen me in nothing but a bra and underwear before. I wasn't concerned. I pulled on the oversized shirt and then unbuckled my jeans. Both boys were whispering and didn't make a note of my change of clothes.

"Are you both sleeping in here?"

"Absolutely, beautiful," Blue responded. His dimpled smile was intoxicating and suspicious. His ordinarily neat crimson hair was messy and laid haphazardly around his masculine jaw. I would bet he was as tired as me. Neither of us slept much on nights like this.

I closed the door a smidge and shuffled towards the size-able dark bed. The minute my knees hit the bottom of the bed, my body gave out. I laid on my stomach with a relieved groan. Decimus chuckled and grasped my waist. He hauled me up to the center of the silky sheets that were warm from the boys' proximity.

"Nighty night, Vegas," Blue cooed. His long pale arm wrapped around my waist as his muscular chest pressed into my back. My head buried into Decimus's side as he began to gently massage my scalp. The scent of sea salt and cinnamon floated around me in comforting waves. Decimus whispered something softly in Greek before the darkness consumed me.

2

VEGAS

I was immediately aware of the heavy warmth that overwhelmed my body. Before I even opened my eyes, I knew Kodiak was wrapped around my waist with his head buried into my stomach. He was an absolutely massive man and no one else emitted body heat quite as he did. He was very bear-like and not just in name.

"Kodiak," I complained while squinting open my left eye. I was right. A large head of soft chocolate brown hair was nuzzled into my bare stomach. Always my bare stomach. Even if I wore a sweater or multiple layers, the man would find a way to push it up and away. Decimus's light snores were to my right and Blue's even breathing to my left. I wasn't worried about waking them. Kodiak, though? He could be woken.

"Vegas," he mumbled a complaint. His usual tanned skin was pale, eyeglasses loose on the bed. Despite his usual gruffness, Kodiak was a total teddy bear at heart. A large green-eyed teddy bear that *totally had a fever.*

"Kodi," I whispered, shaking his broad shoulders. I could tell he had been out hiking last night. His shirt was wrinkled, and he smelled faintly of pine. Those large hands clasped my waist in a tightening vise grip.

Shit. His forehead was so hot and feverish.

"Deci," I murmured. The jerk just rolled over. I tried to not ogle at his back muscles. When had he taken off his shirt?

As if summoned from the heavens, my bedroom door opened to reveal a very sleepy Cosimo. I snorted at the lean, yet very fit man's floppy black hair and bright crystalline eyes. In his hand, he held a blanket and pillow, which meant only one thing – he had come to cuddle.

Do you see what I mean about my room? You can't make this shit up.

"Could you grab me the thermometer? Kodiak has a fever," I mumbled. The sleepy Spanish man nodded and shuffled into the bathroom. Cosimo looked every bit the foreigner he was. Despite being put in the American foster care system at fifteen, he had initially grown up in Spain. When his family moved here and were tragically lost in a fire, he was sent to Ohio to live with us.

He handed me the thermometer and rolled onto the bed. His head rested against Blue's shoulder for barely a second before his snores joined Deci's own. I shook my head at the pile of puppies before I lifted Kodiak's chin and forced his mouth to make a fish face. Despite his growling, I slipped the contraption under his tongue and turned it on.

"Shit, Kodiak," I murmured. "You gotta wake up. You have a 102-degree fever."

The shithead groaned and tightened his grip on my skin once more. I let out a troubled sigh before ruffling his hair gently in a soothing motion. Cosimo muttered something in Spanish before rolling into Blue further. The heat around me increased from simmer to sauté.

"Grover!" I called out in a raspy voice. It was loud enough that Kodiak groaned. Cosimo mumbled some choice English curse words and Deci frowned in his sleep. Blue? He kept sleeping.

"Morning, Angel." Grover shot me his charming smile while leaning in the doorway of my bedroom. He was decidedly hungover and still dressed from the night before. His short dark auburn hair was sticking up in a million different directions, and his sharp masculine jawline was covered in a dark shadow. The most noticeable thing about him, though? The warm chocolate-colored eye that was surrounded by a huge fucking black bruise.

"Where the fuck did you get that bruise?" I growled out. His eyes darkened as he cleared his expression.

"You called?" he responded, ignoring my question.

I narrowed my eyes and motioned to Kodiak. "He has a 102-degree fever. Could you move him to his bedroom while I go grab some medicine?"

Grover ruffled his hair in a sleepy gesture. "Why don't you leave him here, though? It's where he will end up anyway. Even if you move him."

It was true. Kodiak had a massive problem with accepting any change in his daily schedule. Since the start of college, he had always found his way to sleeping in my bed. That probably wouldn't change anytime soon.

"Fine. Help me get out of bed."

He flashed a brilliant smile and walked over to Decimus's side of the bed. With careful movements, Grover was able to lift me out of Kodiak's hold. I pressed a kiss to my sick grizzly bear's head and looked up at Grover.

"Are you going to tell me about the bruise?"

He rubbed the back of his neck and flushed a shade of pink. Ah, shit. Maybe I didn't want to know. Honestly, I didn't. I'd decided. I could tell him no. I mean shit, what if he was coming back from a one night stand? I hadn't even considered that possibility.

"I kissed a girl, and her boyfriend freaked."

Damn it.

Ignoring the surge of jealousy working its way through my body, I responded. "Did you know she had a boyfriend?"

"Yes."

"Why the fuck did you do it then?" I whisper yelled. It's a thing.

He shrugged and looked away. It was clear he wasn't telling me something. I wasn't okay with that at all. Did I have time to deal with it currently? No.

"Fine," I snapped, harsher than I should have. "Be ready to tell me tonight, though. Do you need anything from the store?"

He shook his head and followed me out of the darkened bedroom. I could tell he was feeling down, but I couldn't find it in myself to move on just yet. I was halfway downstairs before I realized that I was still in my sleepwear. Grover had walked into the kitchen to grab some water for Kodiak and himself.

"Shit," I mumbled.

"Here." He tossed me the pair of athletic joggers that he had been wearing only a minute ago. I caught them with a questioning glance.

"I didn't sleep with anyone, angel. I've literally been at the bar all night," he said, raising his hands in defense. I felt terrible because I knew Grover didn't like negative attention. Then again, a small part of my jealousy was much too upset to care. Petty, Vegas. Very petty.

I offered a soft smile, slipped them on, and tightened the waist. He chuckled at the oversized fit and moved toward the stairs – slowly. I may or may not have checked out his cute, boxer clad butt. The man was muscular and looked like a movie star. Sue me.

"Morning," a smooth, husky voice stated from behind me. I turned to see Bandit, stealthy as ever, standing by the door. His coat was on, and his other hand held the car keys. Clearly, he planned on coming with. I never really understood how he predicted my actions to such a great extent but chalked it up to mind reading.

I shrugged on a large oversized jacket and boots. My hug was enough of a greeting for Bandit. With no words, we began trailing down the driveway in the brisk early morning weather. For a Saturday morning, 10 a.m. was like the ass-crack of dawn for our family. My blurry eyes trailed to Bandit, our stealthy thief, who had already started our second family car with the automatic start. Smart man.

"How sick is he?" Bandit asked quietly while opening my door. Out of the two cars that we owned, this one was far nicer. Our older Lincoln Navigator fits most of our group, but the boys had picked out a newer sedan as well. They complained and worried about my safety when I wasn't driving with one of them, so this was our compromise. I yawned while running a hand through my silver-blonde hair.

"A 102-degree fever," I groaned in response. "Which reminds me, let's pick up double of everything. They are all sleeping in my bed like a pile of puppies, so the sickness is sure to multiply."

Bandit nodded. "I'll make soup for the week and grab some tea. We can put some herbal mix-ins for those of us that refuse to admit when we are sick."

I chuckled at that. He clearly was referring to Decimus and me. We liked to pretend that we were perfectly healthy until we were dragging ourselves across the ground. Even then, maybe we were just tired, ever consider that?

We pulled into the Walmart parking lot and found a spot near the door. I was glad Bandit had driven because my eyes were only half-open. Case in point? Bandit's quick save kept me from colliding with a parked car. His large hand wrapped around mine and continued its warming effect long into the store. Maybe this was why everyone thought I was with all of them? Not that those boys did anything at all to dispel such rumors. No. Instead, it was "our girl Vegas."

It was simultaneously horrible and cute. Trust me, I know. I confuse myself with these feelings.

Although, Bandit and I looked far more similar than anyone else in our family. Except for the height and his slightly more feline features, we could have easily been related. Our skin was a similar shade of porcelain and our hair a silver blonde. While mine reached my lower back, his hair was cut short to showcase his vast collection of black gauges and piercings.

"Grab two baskets." I nudged Bandit into action.

Our trips to Walmart were usually extensive. All of the boys had part-time jobs while in school. Despite our academic scholarships, we had no choice but to work for extra expenses like this. I had attempted to search for a job but was promptly told no. Apparently, the boys believed I had enough responsibility. That rule didn't apply to Lucida, which pissed me off. Then again, Lucida was the only member of the Ravens who lived separately. She had wanted a space away from the "extreme testosterone," as she put it. I couldn't blame her. It was a lot to deal with. Personally, I loved it.

After our baskets were filled with over the counter medicine, cough drops, tissues, and tea, we began our walk to the grocery section. I handed the extra basket to Bandit so he could select his ingredients for the soup. I didn't know shit about cooking and didn't pretend to. Bandit, on the other hand, was a fantastic cook and the only one I trusted to prepare more than a frozen pizza.

It was around aisle sixteen when the worst voice *ever* called out to me. Fuck. Clearly, my arch-nemesis didn't take the weekends off. Bandit let out a quiet growl that surprised me as my eyes found K and A. No, I am not at all making this up. The Letters were a group of *children* at our school that went by letters because names were too *jejune*.

"Bandit and Vegas," K hissed while stalking down the aisle. I was always surprised at how popular these guys were. Don't get me wrong. They were an attractive bunch. They wore perfectly pressed shirts and expensive shoes. They drove luxury cars and vibrated with an energy that I didn't completely understand. It attracted a lot of people to them. Yet, none of that made up for their shit personalities.

"It's too fucking early for this," I sighed despondently while leaning into Bandit.

"Where's the crew?" A asked curiously. Out of the two, he was more muscular. I tried to avoid him more than the others. There was sick energy that rolled off his perfectly baby smooth skin.

What fucking beauty products do these boys use? Jesus.

"At home," Bandit responded, but there was tension in his words. Unfortunately, Bandit wasn't very outspoken. It was a feature that led to him being walked on throughout most of high school. He did, however, have a particular bit of hatred and strength reserved for these assholes. I felt his hand tighten around mine. A took note with interest.

"Aren't you two fucking siblings?" he asked with malice.

"Is that what you're into, Vegas?" K chuckled. "Guess we need to be family to fuck her."

"Fuck you," I snarled. Bandit shook with anger but didn't say anything. Instead, he pulled me from the aisle with increased strength. Our strides were long, and the assholes didn't follow.

"Sorry," Bandit murmured at the register. "I know you don't like to walk away from fights, but I didn't think it was one I could win."

My passive stealth man.

I nudged his shoulder while he scanned the items. "It's okay, really."

His bright spring green eyes met mine for a heartbeat before he nodded and continued. Once we had checked out, I grasped his hand firmly in mine. I didn't want him to feel guilty for walking away. Hell. It was the mature thing to do! We had enough fighters and hotheads in our group. I liked his passive, peacekeeping nature. We needed more of that.

"Are you going to tell them what happened?"

I groaned and adjusted the heat as we drove home. I could feel a chill seeping into my bones, and I prayed I wasn't getting sick. I was not a happy camper when sick and made everyone else equally as miserable.

"I suppose," I mumbled. "Rocket and Deci are going to flip."

"And Blue," he sighed. Fuck. Blue hated them even more. Booker and Cosimo were my passionate and expressive pair. Bandit and Grover were my pacifists. Usually. I say usually because I knew they all had a temper to some extent. You didn't come from the backgrounds they did and not learn how to stick up for yourself.

The other four in our group? Fucking knuckleheads. I could easily guarantee Blue and Deci would go looking for a fight. Kodiak was usually up in the air, but he hated The Letters and was a tad overprotective. As in overprotective to the point of following me to each and every one of my dates. Ever. Rocket though? He grunted and growled more than he spoke. I always noticed odd primal energy that seemed to roll off him in waves.

The house was quiet and dark as we pulled up. I grabbed a bag and followed up after Bandit. It was near noon now, and the house was slowly waking. I ignored the disaster that was our living room and walked upstairs with the medicine. Bandit went to start the soup.

"Vegas," a deep rough voice called out.

"Morning, sickie," I laughed at Kodiak.

It was clear that everyone had woken and stumbled to their own bedrooms, probably out of fear of getting sick. Kodiak laid in bed, right in the center, and gave me a pathetic small grunt. I snickered.

My room was beautiful, especially in the early afternoon light. It hadn't escaped my notice that the place the boys had put the most effort in fixing up was the one they ended up in most nights. The walls were a beautiful shade of indigo that Booker had picked out. When I asked him about the color choice, he had mumbled something about my eye color. I had thought the gesture was incredibly sweet.

That was my boys for you. Absolute sweethearts. Even the assholes.

I moved to the far wall and opened all of the windows to let in the autumn breeze. Kodiak was sorting through the bag of medicine and making grunts of approval. I pulled open my dark wood dresser and grabbed some clothing for the day. Except I didn't get very far.

"Kodiak," I chuckled. He was carrying me back to the

giant bed. The sheets were a soft silver and lavender that complimented my plush carpet.

"You're staying with me all day," he grumbled. "I will *not* be sick alone."

I laughed at that. "But if I get sick, I can't take care of you."

"Well, then, we will both be miserable fucks together."

I didn't bother arguing with him. It was Saturday afternoon. I had absolutely nothing to do. After we snuggled further into the covers, Kodiak wiggled his way to rest his flushed cheek against my stomach. He pushed up my shirt quickly and sighed with contentment. The movement sent a warm tingle of desire through me. The habit had always made me feel good, but lately, something had changed.

I knew I was healing from what had happened before. With that healing came an array of emotions I wasn't positive I was ready to handle.

"Love you," he mumbled out. His snores began almost right away. I was happy to have gotten a dose of medicine in him before he passed out.

"Love you, too," I whispered before closing my own eyes.

3

BLUE

J stood in the doorway of the master bedroom, watching them sleep with absolute fascination. If anyone held her like that, outside of the Ravens, they would be dead. Not metaphorically. No. They would be six feet under, pushing daisies. Instead, the scene in front of me filled me with immense satisfaction and happiness.

Our family was perfect. She was the center of our dangerous little world. A silver moon that shed light on a fathomless night. It was precisely how it fucking should be. Forever.

"Blue," Bandit called from down the hallway. I snapped my head to look at our silver-haired brother. Sometimes I wondered why he and Vegas appeared so similar in coloring. It was a very unique hair color to have and not exactly a natural tone.

I looked back at her slim figure one more time before turning to meet him. Her waist-length hair spread out in waves across the pillows. Her purple-blue eyes were shut, framed by thick dark lashes. Her dark red lips parted in exhale. Somehow a bunch of foster kids had landed themselves a radiant silver-haired goddess. The eight of us boys were still counting our lucky fucking stars.

Vegas was *ours*. No part of me shied away from the possession of that thought.

"What's up?" I asked Bandit curiously. I immediately noticed his tense jaw and hardened eyes. Had something happened at the store? Vegas had sounded happy just moments ago. I would know since I had been hanging outside the bedroom like a total creep.

"We ran into K and A at Walmart," he spoke quietly. I could tell his temper was bubbling right underneath the surface. It surprised me.

Bandit was not a fighter. He was calm and very methodical. Even when he had shed blood, which had happened, it had been less aggressive and more like fine art. There was an emptiness to Bandit that seemed to only be filled by Vegas's company. I understood that well, though.

I had no qualms about my dual personality. I had embraced my insanity when it came to Vegas a very long time ago. I had killed for her once and wouldn't think twice about doing it again. It took very little for me to snap, and once I did, there was no going back. Vegas didn't know the depths I had gone to ensure her safety, and I never wanted her to. The urge to protect her was compulsive, nearly feral, and if removing someone from her life would do the trick then so be it. For this reason, I asked the following question.

"What happened?"

As he relayed the incident to me, I felt my body grow rigid and jaw tense. I could feel the rage rolling off me in thick malicious waves. No one talked to Vegas like that. No one implied anything rude or offensive towards her. Ever. Fuck. No one even spoke to her unless we were okay with it. She was ours.

"Bandit," Decimus greeted casually before meeting my eyes. I was sure he saw my anger because of the question that formed on his lips.

"Who?"

"The Letters," I stated with all the calm I could muster. It wasn't much.

"I'll be ready in two," Decimus stated before going to knock on more doors.

"Stay here with Cosimo," I spoke quietly, "Lock up just in case."

Bandit nodded before going to Cosimo's shut door. Hopefully, they would be able to keep Vegas unsuspecting if she woke up.

Grover appeared in the hallway with a faint smirk on his face. He got off on shit like this and I couldn't blame him one fucking bit. I still needed to talk to him about that fucking bruise on his face. I didn't buy the story he had given Vegas, plus it had hurt her fucking feelings. Something I was very much not okay with.

"Rocket, where are they right now?" I asked the other man coming down the hall with Booker. Both looked furious. I made the assumption Decimus had updated them.

"Gym," he nearly barked out. Perfect.

"Don't think we aren't talking about that bruise later," I warned Grover.

Without another word, we left the house. I knew we didn't need all five of us, but no one liked to miss out on shit like this. When Vegas was part of the situation, most of them flat out refused to *not* be part of it.

I knew our relationship with her was unique. The eight of us loved her. She loved each one of us without exception. While we had waited to foster anything romantic until we felt she was ready, none of us had ever squashed the rumors about our group. In fact, we may have encouraged them. It was becoming more difficult to pretend as of late. Everything she did drew us in. I could see the confusion flashing through her beautiful eyes at her change of feelings. I saw it in the way she looked at us and the way she interacted with us. If I ever sensed guilt at all on her part, the game would be over. I would instantly tell her everything about our little plan.

It had been after her first boyfriend in high school that we had come to the conclusion that we would rather share Vegas than to ever let her go. She didn't have to choose because we would always be a family. Vegas was our center. The woman who held a bunch of orphaned boys together. The first and only woman to ever make us feel loved. We had dated other girls before, but from the time we turned sixteen, most of us understood the place Vegas held in our life. It almost felt as though fate had placed us together.

As we pulled in the gym parking lot, I nearly flew out of the car. I could feel the four of them jogging after me. My only goal was the fucking Letters. I moved up the stairs and through the glass doors quickly. Security let out a yell, but I was gone. I figured someone could calm them down later. I didn't give a fuck.

Then I saw A and K. My smile in the mirror set my own hair on edge. I knew the minute they saw me. It was the same minute that my hand gripped A's neck and slammed him into the glass mirror.

"Fuck," K groaned. He let out a guttural sound as Decimus laughed and pressed an elbow into his chest to hold him in place. They knew why I was here. Both of them were silent as I chose my words carefully.

"It seems we need to clarify a few things," I snarled

quietly. I knew we were drawing a crowd, but my three brothers behind us formed a shield from any prying eyes.

"Listen, you stupid fucking human," K snarled. Not for the first time, I felt the air tense with an energy I didn't understand. Who the fuck insults someone by calling them human? Decimus chuckled again before moving his elbow up to K's neck, cutting off any speech. I continued.

"The only reason your entrails aren't painting this fucking room red is that Vegas would feel guilty. She's sweet like that. You don't deserve it. You don't deserve a thought in her head. So let me make myself very clear. You look at her. You think about her. You even breathe the same air as Vegas, and I will gut you."

A snarled. "You can't be fucking serious!"

"I am. I would love nothing more than to slice you open and see your blood spill across the floor. Booker could make a fucking mural out of it. Or, hell, maybe Rocket can use you for his latest experiment, yeah? Didn't you need human test subjects, Rocket? You can keep them locked up in our basement and pull them apart piece by piece."

Rocket offered a dark amused chuckle that had both boys turning paperwhite. It wasn't an idle threat.

"You would get caught," K spoke in a strangled tone.

Decimus chuckled again. "Nah, I'll just make a bonfire out of your fucking corpse."

"So, do we have an understanding, Letters?"

Both boys nodded. I grinned, showing off my deceptive good old boy smile before stepping back. Decimus let go of K at the same time, and both started sucking in oxygen. Grover stepped through and knelt down to eye level with a heaving K.

"Also," he spoke in a soft dark tone. "You tell C that if he ever uses our name to sell drugs, I will end what he started last night."

With that, we left the gym. I could feel a comfortable thrill of excitement pulse through my body. What did it say that scaring them shitless made me happy? Nothing. It said nothing because they deserved it.

"I have a question." Booker grinned.

"What?" Grover asked curiously.

"How did C get a hit on you?"

Grover chuckled, deep and loud. "He didn't. I fell on my way home and hit myself on the edge of a parked car. I was wasted."

We lost it at that. Fucking Grover.

4

VEGAS

"*B*andit." I pinned him with a stare. "Where did they go?"

Bandit, the smug bastard, served soup to a sleepy Kodiak. Cosimo had started to gently massage my shoulders. It didn't help distract me from my current train of thought. I had woken to only the three of them home, which meant one thing.

"You told them," I accused.

"K and A deserve whatever is coming to them," Cosimo murmured. He then began the very distracting act of tracing patterns against my bare arm. He hummed lightly as I felt my body lean back into his intoxicating, exotic scent. Damn him. He was good at this distraction thing.

"Told them what?" Kodiak demanded. Suddenly, he looked less sick. Oh, no.

"Nothing."

The front door opened, and the house filled with the rest of my boys. I offered them an initial, nearly automatic smile, and then swiftly switched it to a scowl. Decimus chuckled while lighting a cigarette.

Blue offered me those fucking dimples and moved to stand on my other side. He pressed a kiss to my temple, and everyone began to pretend like I wasn't scowling. Even Grover grabbed some soup and started talking to Kodiak in a low whisper. Rocket stood with Booker and examined the first coat of paint.

"Boys," I growled quietly. Everyone ignored me.

I looked at a puppy-eyed Cosimo. "*No te preocupes hermosa.*"

"Uh-uh," I shook my head and traveled to the center of the room. I moved my glare over each one of them and prayed it was slightly intimidating. My arms crossed. My foot was two seconds away from tapping.

"Beautiful," Blue whined. "You look too cute when you're mad. We can't have a conversation during your pouting."

"I am not pouting!" I snarled. "I am pissed."

"She looks like a kitten," Booker mumbled while drinking soup.

"I could see that," Bandit added unhelpfully.

"Come on, now. Let's give her something a tad more vicious than a kitten," Decimus offered.

"A fluffy white Arctic fox?" Kodiak suggested after finishing his soup.

Rocket chuckled softly. "I like that better."

I flipped them off and began to stalk up the stairs.

Grover called out. "Come back, angel!"

I maintained my loud footsteps. Screw them. I wasn't even sure I wanted to know for sure, but I wanted the fucking option. Once in my bedroom, my anger dissipated. It was hard to stay mad at them for stuff like this. I knew how defensive and protective I got about my family, so I could hardly blame them for doing the same.

"Luci!" I exclaimed. I had picked up my phone while walking into my spacious room.

"Hunny," she said in that smokey voice of hers. "Are we going to Stools tonight?"

"Yep. Is Miranda in town?"

"No," she sighed. "I'm coming by to get ready, though. Are the boys all home?"

I groaned. "Don't even get me started. They're on my shit list."

She chuckled. "What did they do this time?"

I told her about the run-in with K and A. By the end of the story, she wasn't laughing but yelling curses about those "two dumbfucks." I pulled my ear away and grimaced at the volume.

"Okay, okay," I grinned. "Save my eardrums."

She sighed as my bedroom door opened. Cosimo walked in with that dangerous, sexy swagger he had. His eyes lit up at my smile.

"See you in ten," she finally stated before hanging up.

"What happened to getting ready?" he asked with curiosity. His gemstone eyes were wide and no longer sleepy. Of all my boys, he was the most fascinating to look at. His midnight hair was usually styled to the side but always looked slightly messy and sexy in that way only men could perfect. Currently, he still wore his PJs and looked deliciously relaxed.

"Luci just called," I explained while slipping off my oversized robe. "Plus, I need to shower before getting ready."

Cosimo's eyes burned up my bare legs, now only covered by a loose shirt hitting mid-thigh. I saw an unfamiliar heat fill those crystal eyes. It caused me to make a surprised sound and blush. He locked his gaze on me in a way that made me feel very much like prey. A small smile tilted onto his full lips as he moved forward slowly like a jungle cat.

"Cosimo?" I squeaked.

His muscular body was far more noticeable under his black sleep shirt. It was molded to his shape and nearly as tight as his pants. He always wore his clothes tight. Hell, I would, too, if my body was that fit and lean.

"Vegas," he purred softly in a near whisper. "You could tempt the sinless."

I felt my breathing hitch as desire unfurled in my stomach. Where the hell was this coming from? I mean I was so, *so* not complaining, but fuck. Give a girl some warning.

"What?" I whispered. His hands, rough and warm, grasped my hips gently as he pinned me to the wall. I found myself staring up into his stargaze and wishing he would kiss me. Something brightened in his eyes as he smiled. It was as if he had come to a realization.

"You want me," he murmured. It wasn't cocky. It was surprised.

"What gave it away?" I licked my bottom lip nervously before biting down on it.

Cosimo pressed a heated kiss to my forehead before stepping back. I instantly felt the loss. Did he not want me? Had I misread him pinning me to the wall? Because *that* happens often, right?

I must have been transparent because he stepped back into my space and lifted my chin. "Remove that pout from your delicious lips before you tempt me to break."

"Why did you stop?" I whispered. With anyone else except Cosimo and maybe Bandit, I would have been embarrassed by my question.

He groaned and pressed his forehead to mine. "I have to do something first. Believe me, though, I am not putting the brakes on this because of you. I just hadn't realized you were ready."

"Huh?" I asked with utter confusion.

He grinned, pressing a kiss to my forehead. "Nothing. Now go get your sexy ass ready."

With that, Cosimo was gone. I was officially confused beyond belief. What did he have to do first? Ready for what? It was just a kiss, right? Also, he thought my ass was sexy? Cool. Very cool.

I shook my head in an attempt to declutter my brain. It worked just enough to get my ass moving. I went through the motions of turning on my Bluetooth speaker, courtesy of Rocket, and began blasting Meg Myers.

As I stepped into the shower and locked the bathroom door, I heard Luci arrive. I made sure to make my shower short to conserve water. The act of showering in a household of nine was a feat in itself. I had scheduled it out so that half the boys showered in the morning and half at night. So far, we had only run into problems on the weekends.

"Ve!" Luci called out. I stepped out of the bathroom in my lavender cotton robe and began towel drying my hair.

"Hey, babes," I smiled. As usual, Luci looked colorful. Her jaw-length hair was springy with curls and colored a bubblegum pink this week. I loved the bright colors against her mocha skin.

"What do you think?" she asked while shaking her curls.

"I absolutely love it," I said after inspection. I loved a bright color pallette on Luci. Me? Not so much.

"I could dye your hair," she whispered conspiratorially.

"No!" Blue shouted from the hallway. I chuckled at his love for my hair. Literally, it was more of an obsession. I sometimes wondered if he liked my hair more than me.

Luci rolled her eyes and began pulling items from her bag. While my best friend and I were similar in height and build, our sense of fashion couldn't be more different. I was focused on comfort almost every hour of the day. I owned jeans, hoodies, and sneakers. I had made it my mission to perfect the art of wearing an oversized hoodie without looking homeless. It helped that I wore my boys' clothes a majority of the time. Luci, on the other hand, was always dressed up in bright patterns. After a few years of being disappointed in my outfit choices, we had come to a compromise. She could pick out my outfits when we went out *if* I could wear whatever I wanted the rest of the time. Usually, she pinpointed my style pretty well, and tonight she didn't disappoint.

"Oh," I cooed at one of the many dresses from her closet. "Pretty."

Luci shut the door and began to get ready. Her process was more extensive than my own, but I made sure to take my time tonight. Something about Cosimo's words made me think tonight would be different. Or I hoped it would. It was getting difficult to ignore how I felt about these boys. *That* was the problem though. My feelings were multiple, not singular.

I slipped into my silky grey bra as fear invaded my mind. What would happen to our group? If I kissed one of them, it wouldn't ruin everything, right? I couldn't lose them to something so silly, right? My features paled.

I shook the thoughts and pulled on my dress for tonight. It was bold but still comfortable. The back dipped low in a geometric shape to the top of my ass, but the front had a standard wide neckline. The sleeves were long and tight, which matched the rest of the shape. The dark satin material was shining in the evening sunset as I looked myself over.

"Hot damn!" Luci whistled. "You look fucking great. If I were straight, you would have convinced me to test the waters."

I chuckled at that. "You're crazy."

"Let me do your hair!" She scrambled forward in her electric blue mini dress. I sat down to let her work my long wet hair into some type of style. After a half an hour of work, Luci had created a silver snowfall of curls that began at the back of my head and cascaded down my shoulder. I had to admit, I looked fucking great.

When the boys called up, Luci scrambled to lock the door. She chuckled and began finishing up my makeup. It was light. A line of dark liner and soft pink lipstick. I finally slipped on strappy crystal heels as a knock sounded. Luci unlocked the door. My focus was on adjusting my dress at the time, so the silence from our unknown knocker didn't seem odd. Then Luci burst out laughing.

I lifted my eyes and blushed ten shades of red. Maybe even purple.

Impressive, Vegas.

Blue's denim eyes were filled with heat, and his mouth was frozen as if he was going to say something. Decimus grinned and looked over my body like the predator he was and, apparently, the prey I had become. Grover's warm brown eyes seemed unusually dark with something that looked a lot like desire. Each of their looks made me equally nervous and thrilled.

"What are you idiots doing?" Kodiak grumbled while pushing through the door. I knew I was in trouble the minute he saw me. Not the trouble I wanted either.

His dark green eyes looked me up and down. Instantly

his jaw tightened, and his eyes darkened ten shades to a near black. A deep rumble echoed from his chest before he turned on his heel and let out a curse.

"Get her a fucking hoodie!" he yelled. Blue broke out into a huge grin.

"What the hell?" Luci asked while laughing so hard she was holding her sides.

"Does he not like the dress?" I asked curiously. He had never commented on my outfit choices before.

Decimus chuckled. "Oh, baby, I don't think that's the issue."

"You look gorgeous," Blue commented softly. His appreciative tone made me blush, and Luci shook her head. She looked like she was trying to hold back her laughter now.

"All right, let's go," she sighed with amusement. Her hand slipped into mine as we moved past the boys.

"I wasn't joking about the hoodie!" Kodiak yelled from the bottom of the stairs.

"What?" Booker asked looking up. He blushed.

Bandit said, "Oh."

"Shit, Vegas," Cosimo called from the couch.

"See this bullshit, Vegas?" Luci whispered with amusement. "This is why I like women."

"What the fuck are all of you being so loud about?" Rocket growled into the room. He stopped and looked down at me. I kid you not. He swayed on the spot.

Those sparkling grey eyes darkened, and he barked. "Someone get her a fucking hoodie."

Okay, this time even I laughed. My boys could be slightly protective.

5

BANDIT

*M*y fingers curled around Vegas's long pale fingers. It wasn't a handhold as much as a lifeline. She was the strength I needed to get through tonight. Actually, she was the strength I needed to get through any night.

I was anti-social to an extreme. Except when it came to the family. They weren't a social experience though. No, they were my life. They accepted me despite my hatred of larger social gatherings. No one at home ever made me feel at odds with my nature, especially Vegas.

However, my hatred for socialization had resulted in a handy skillset. I was a stellar thief. I could perform a sleight of hand like no one else I knew. When needed, I moved in and out of space quickly and efficiently. You wouldn't know I had been there until I was long gone. As we made our way through Stools, I noticed multiple openings to lift wallets and costume jewelry. It was second nature.

There was energy buzzing under my skin in response to Vegas's close proximity. It made this atmosphere bearable. At the same time, it was hard to be around her. That dress was a walking bullseye. Every single, hormonal college student noticed the natural sway of her hips and curiously bright eyes. Every single one.

They didn't deserve to look at her. *Hell.* I barely deserved to look at her. If it weren't for my belief that the eight of us could make her happy, I wouldn't expect her to stay with me. I was a slight pushover at best and weak at worst. Even today at Walmart, I had felt every protective instinct coming alive under my skin because of The Letters' words. I hadn't acted though. I didn't trust myself enough to place her in a dangerous situation. That was the problem, wasn't it? I was so worried about what I would do that I did nothing.

"Do you want anything to drink?" I murmured in a whisper near her ear. A shiver raced through her, and those indigo eyes turned on me. I nearly groaned at the way her lips parted.

Vegas licked her lips lightly, and she leaned in. "Can you get me a glass of wine?"

"Absolutely." I pressed a gentle kiss to her nose. Blue nodded toward our booth and led Vegas away from the crowded bar. The crowd began to swarm in her absence. I pushed toward the bar.

"What can I get you?" The bartender was young. He looked familiar, but I couldn't place his name. Unfortunately, Blue was far better at that than me. I knew my place on the team, and it had nothing to do with people.

"One glass of prosecco and vodka on ice." I tossed him a twenty. My forearms were bent over the smooth modern surface as people crowded around me. I looked forward to being back at the booth. While Vegas wasn't aware of it, we took extra caution whenever we brought her out. The security around the room was nearly imperceptible. It was the one stipulation for our new job.

The boss hadn't thought it was odd to request extra security for one of our team members. In fact, he had seemed to agree with it. I groaned despondently. Another aspect Vegas would need to be informed of. I felt awful keeping so many aspects of our life secret. Blue claimed it was necessary. I didn't agree.

She was strong. So incredibly strong. If anyone could understand our position, it would be her. It wouldn't change anything. If anything, she could help us. She was supposed to be helping us.

When I had first arrived at the large foster care home in rural Ohio, I hadn't known what to expect. My experiences up until that point in time had all been rather depressing. I had been homeless and living in cheap motels with my mom for as long as I could remember. She had been a strung-out junkie. I had seen everything from my mother whoring herself out to finding her lifeless body in an alley we had inhabited. It had been that day I had come across a man, an undercover cop, that brought me to a local station for help.

My social experiences up until that point were minimal, and my schooling had been anything but traditional. I had no belongings and no family. When they informed me I would be leaving my temporary housing to travel to Ohio, I felt nothing. I had been skinny and probably had looked like a junkie myself.

I stepped out of the ugly minivan that Carol had transported me in. Carol was the local social worker and an annoyingly loud woman. The air had been cold, and my second-hand sweater did little to keep me warm. Then again, I had grown numb to most things.

"Ve!" a thick accent called out as Carol turned her eyes to the large Victorian house before us. It was an impressive house. Then

again, it wasn't an alley, so it was the best fucking house in the world.

"Hi! My name is Vegas," a wind chime voiced. I flinched back, and my eyes rounded on a fairy. No joke. Wings and all.

"Vegas?" I asked quietly. I heard Carol gasp. Oh, shit. She had never heard my voice, that's awkward.

"I know." The little girl pouted her pink lips. "It's totally stupid."

I smiled. She was perfect. Her silver hair matched mine and surrounded her like a blanket. A pair of large lilac eyes took up most of her face. They happened to match her purple wings as well.

"Ve!" a thick Russian accent demanded. I didn't like the tone of her voice and felt my hand close around Vegas's slim fingers. I felt strength push through me. I felt stronger than I ever had in my life.

Carol laughed. "Good to see you, Vivian."

My eyes fell upon a large woman with a massive mop of curly hair and dough covered hands. Despite her initial tone, I didn't sense anything violent or angry about her. Vegas giggled quietly before moving to stand directly next to me. Odd energy buzzed between the two of us as a beautiful silver mist coated our arms.

What the heck was going on? Neither of the adults commented on it.

"Carol." The woman nodded before turning her grey eyes to mine. "And who do we have here?"

I felt my throat close up. I didn't know my name. What type of kid doesn't have a name? My mom had always just called me "boy."

Vegas squeezed my hand and stood on her toes to whisper in my ear. "If you don't like your name, just make one up."

Her words were my strength. I nodded and stuck out my hand. "My name is Bandit."

Vivan smiled and met my hand with hers. "Welcome home, Bandit."

I think I picked the name because of the raccoons I had watched in the alleyways at night. They always stole garbage like I stole wallets for my mom. It had been the one thing she had praised me for. Had she actually been surprised by my ability to be practically invisible?

I knew Vivan meant that the house was my new home, but my eyes were stuck on the fairy next to me. She smiled and tugged on my hand. In that instant, at that exact moment, I knew my soul belonged to her. Vegas had given me a name. I was a real person to her.

No. This house wasn't my home. She was my home.

"Here," I whispered to the woman whose existence defined my own. She was seated next to Luci and had left a spot open for me. No one had sat in it. They all knew I needed her on nights like this.

It was moments like that. Moments where I had no doubt that our plan would work. We just had to finish this job, and we could tell her. We could make a plan for after college and focus on us. My hand slipped into her small palm as she blinded me with a smile.

"Thanks, Bandit," she whispered. While she continued her conversation with Luci, I traced light patterns across her palm. My small smile grew at the blush that blasted her high cheekbones. After what Cosimo had mentioned today, I wouldn't hold back as much as before. She didn't seem unreceptive. In fact, I could see her biting her soft lips gently before casting me a coy smile.

I had a brilliant idea then. I could ask her to dance and try to kiss her. Surely, with how crowded it was, we would be pressed close together, right? It could work. I was about to ask her to dance when the sprinklers went off.

VEGAS

"Shit!" Luci screamed. I let out a bark of laughter and threw my head back. This was such a fucking mess. So fucking typical. My silver hair had turned very heavy upon getting wet, and it was now slowly sliding out of the updo. Blue watched it with satisfaction as if the updo had somehow personally offended him.

Apparently, someone had lit up in a nearby booth and set the fucking velvet on fire. Idiot. The fire itself was put out, but that hadn't stopped chaos from erupting. My initial instinct was to grab Bandit. He had a terrible fear of crowds.

The room emptied as water flooded the marble dance floor. I hadn't moved from where Bandit clutched my waist tightly. Both of us were soaked and smiling. Luci sat with a terrible scowl on her face. The rest of our group stood around our booth protectively. No one made it close enough to even see past the wall that was my boys. It was another reason I assumed there was no actual threat, or the boys would have hauled our asses out of here.

"You okay?" I asked my silver-haired introvert in a soft whisper.

He grinned and shook his hair. It sprayed water on my face and caused a very unladylike shriek to emerge from my mouth. Someone groaned from the wall of men and Bandit smiled even more as those green eyes sparked with trouble.

"What?" I asked, looking up and meeting Rocket's steely gaze. He was soaked but shrugged off his suit coat. Rocket forced my arms through it. He leveled Bandit with a knowing gaze.

"I didn't make the sprinklers go off, Rocket," Bandit chuckled with innocent doe eyes. What the heck was going on?

"You're distracting them with your *wet dream* look," Luci whispered dramatically. Her makeup streamed down her face. Her bubble gum pink curls dripped with water. I chuckled assuming that was close to what I looked like.

"Can we go?" I whined while leaning against Bandit. His warm palm grasped my hip gently and smoothed it with the softest touch. I sighed into his embrace and felt my eyes close. He was like a space heater. We stayed plastered together for some time. Eventually, I felt someone lift me off Bandit. I assumed we were going to the car. I hoped we were. I couldn't bring myself to open my eyes. I was exhausted.

"Someone needs to check out that lead," Luci whispered softly. Lead?

"I will," Kodiak's rough voice sounded near my ear.

"No," Blue spoke softly. "You're sick."

Kodiak rumbled out something incoherent. I felt my eyes flutter shut. They opened slightly as we got into the car. I nestled into Kodiak's chest, and after breathing in his pine scent, the darkness of sleep consumed me. Someone pressed a soft kiss to my nose.

6

BLUE

"What the fuck?" I snarled. It was nearly four hours after the incident at Stools. I stood looking over our surveillance of entrances and exits. The pictures were far better than the grainy ass footage their older cameras had captured. The comparison was laughable.

"I'm glad we pulled that alarm when we did," Decimus sighed. "Sprinklers were a nice touch." He lit a cigarette, and I bit back my retort. The fucker knew how terrible they were for him.

"And you're positive they didn't distribute at all?"

"Not positive, but pretty damn sure. Except, it's odd. None of those sellers are known or listed in any of our files. They seem like kids on their first route."

"We have to figure out who their distributor is," I mumbled in a distracted tone. I could feel the exhaustion weighing down on my shoulders. It had been a long fucking day.

"We'll get there, Blue," Decimus sighed. He stood up, put out his light, and trailed to the stairs. I nodded before sitting down at the table. I wanted nothing more than to crawl up to Vegas's room. I knew that was where he was headed. I forced myself to look through the pictures one more time.

I sat there until my ass grew numb. The dawn emerged, and birds woke before I forced myself to put the file away. My feet grew heavy as I trudged toward the master bedroom. If it had been up to me, I would have built a huge fucking bed for all nine of us to sleep on. It was where we all ended up anyway.

The bedroom door stood open, and the sight made me exceptionally happy. I believed Cosimo when he suggested she was ready. He was exceptionally good at reading body language. English hadn't been his first language, so he had often relied on his knowledge of nonverbal communication. I hoped he was right. I was done waiting to kiss Vegas. Done waiting to claim her. I wanted the entire fucking school to know she was ours, in every capacity.

Decimus and Bandit both slept as bookends to her slim form. Kodiak, as usual, was wrapped around her center. I knew Booker and Rocket would be asleep in their shared bedroom. They were less comfortable with expressing phys-icality. Cosimo and Grover would both be in their separate bedrooms. The second slept better in his own space, and the first was a fucking blanket hog.

I felt a pang of guilt. I knew Bandit was correct. The fact that we were hiding our job from Vegas didn't bode well for her possible trust in us. I promised myself to tell her once I thought it was safe enough. She had so much self-imposed responsibility that I didn't want to add to it. I wanted to wrap her in a tight cocoon and lock her up. It was possessive and archaic. I didn't give a fuck. My first priority was protecting her.

We had always claimed that Vegas was our leader. She

was. She was also so much more than that. She was our center. Every day she focused so much on our well being that she rarely had time for herself. I wanted that to change. I wanted her always smiling, even if it was unrealistic.

It had always been that way. I had always craved that smile. The carefree nature of it was absolutely addicting. After a few more moments of thought, I turned and walked toward my bedroom. It was a simple space. It mostly consisted of pictures I had taken. Many of them, obsessively so, were of Vegas. I didn't need pictures to remember that face correctly. I had a partially photographic memory, and hers was the brightest face of them all. Still, it felt good to have her around.

My sheets were chilled as I pulled them around my boxer clad figure. I let out a groan and fell into an easy breathing pattern. Before long, my dreams began to manifest.

"Blue," an annoying voice, whined. "Hang out with us!"

It was the first day at my new school. My new school was simply one of a million. Every few months, from as early as I could remember, I had been shuffled around. Now I was in Ohio at a small religious school. I had only arrived yesterday and had instantly been bombarded with directions by some large Russian woman. Vivian was it? I couldn't tell you her name, just what she looked like.

After switching schools so many times, my ability to interact in social situations had become well-tuned. My eyes scanned the group ahead of me, and I found neither of the two people I was most curious about. Where were the two silver-haired children I had seen leave the house before me? I knew they were around my age and Vivian had mentioned the boy had only arrived recently as well.

How were they friends already? Would they want to be my friend?

"Blue," the voice whined again. I looked down at the nondescript face. After memorizing so many faces, they began to blend together so this girl was no different. Finally, I caught silver. My eyes narrowed on the duet by the swings. They were whispering with both of their heads down.

"Who are they?"

The girl sneered. "Them? That's Vegas and some new kid."

Another boy spoke up. "Vegas is super weird dude. She always draws these freaky pictures of messed up fairy tales."

I felt a weird pang of anger surge through my chest. My eyes locked on the large kid in front of me. He realized his mistake fairly quickly. Without another word, I left the group and trailed towards the duet.

"Hi," I called out.

Both heads shot up. I instantly locked eyes with the boy. His face was more unusual than I was used to. I had been in many foster homes and had never seen someone like him. His features reminded me of a cat, very angular and sharp. His bright green eyes were shadowed with pain. I understood pain. I could be friends with someone who understood pain.

"Hello!" a wind chime voice spoke, drawing my attention to the girl. I felt another weird pang surge through my chest. This wasn't anger though. No, this was something different. Concern possibly?

She was so small. So delicate and little. I wasn't a terribly huge kid, and neither was this other boy, but we were much bigger than her. How did she stay safe? What if someone pushed her on the playground? What if there was a strong wind and it knocked her over? A million different terrible possibilities ran through my head. I settled on one thought.

I had to make sure none of that happened.

I looked over at the other boy. He nodded, and under-standing washed over me. He knew. He could help me. It was a big job, and she was terribly delicate looking. There was some-thing special about her. Something so unique I would never be able to forget it. I just couldn't tell you what that special thing was. Still, it reminded me of a flame in a dark room. Comforting and warm.

"Do you not talk?" she asked with a confused arched brow. Her intense gaze struck me as all-seeing. I bet she was one of those people that noticed everything. Like me.

The other boy smiled and stuck out his hand. "Bandit."

I grinned at my new silver-haired friend. "Blue."

"Oh, my God," the girl sighed dramatically. "I totally said hi first."

I turned to face her and offered my hand. "Terrible apologies, Vegas."

"How do you know my name?!" she exclaimed with rapt interest. "Are you a mind reader? I have told Vivi a million times that they exist. Just like my fire..."

Bandit chuckled while clapping a hand over her mouth. The chuckle turned to a worried gasp as she tumbled off her swing. I wasn't positive how I moved so fast, but I found myself catching her. I straightened her up and nodded to Bandit. She was proving my point already.

"Sorry," she grinned. "Vivi says I have two left feet."

"What does that even mean?" Bandit wondered out loud. "Is that possible?"

I chuckled and sat down. I could feel the other children staring but didn't care. I had found my friends, and I was oddly protective of them. I would do my best to be a good friend and protect our silver-haired girl.

I wasn't positive how long I had slept. Suddenly my eyes opened, and the world around me was bathed in gold. I looked around to find the sunset peeking through the large window on my bedroom's far wall.

"Morning," a soft voice mumbled. My eyes found the warm, soft body pressed to mine. Instantly, I became acutely aware of Vegas's lack of clothing. I could feel her light sleep-wear but did that shit even count as clothing?

"How long have we been sleeping?" I asked quietly. My hand went to her face and a frown formed on my own. Shit. She had a fever.

"Beautiful," I shook her shoulders gently. Those long lashes closed further as a little frown created a cute expression on her beautiful face.

With smooth movements, I adjusted Vegas in my arms without disrupting her now even breathing. At the same time, I attempted to ignore how hot her body looked in just soft cotton shorts and a tank top. It had been getting harder to ignore the physical effect she had on me, and almost as if she knew, the little minx had started wearing less and less around the house. On the one hand, it was hell for all of us to look but not touch. On the other, I was pleased that she felt comfortable in her own skin. Once in the hallway, my path to the master bedroom had me nearly running into Decimus.

"Finally up?" Decimus asked from his doorway.

"Get me the thermometer and medicine," I rasped. My voice always sounded like shit before coffee in the morning.

"What?" Decimus frowned. Then he saw Vegas's flushed face and nodded resolutely.

Once I had her set up in bed, I gathered her mass of hair. I pulled it into a messy bun that kept it off her neck. In high school, she had taught me how to braid her hair, and I had been obsessed ever since. I made a point to touch it as much as possible. It had been the first quality I had noticed about her.

"Aw, poor baby," Cosimo cooed from the bedroom door. The lazy shit tumbled into bed next to her and promptly fell asleep. I swore he could fall asleep anywhere. He was the equivalent of a house cat.

"I got it," Decimus brought in the thermometer and an array of different medicine.

"Beautiful," I encouraged her to wake up slightly.

"No." She frowned with a slight scowl.

"Baby," my voice graveled. As cute as I found it, I was worried about her and wanted to see just how sick she was. Finally, her lips relaxed, and I began taking her temperature. I was concerned about how warm she felt and the way her eyes kept fluttering shut.

"When was the last time you ate or drank something?"

Those cute little lips scrunched. "I don't know."

"Bandit!" Decimus called from the door.

"What's up? Oh, shit," Bandit whispered, "Kodiak is already looking better today, so maybe it won't last?"

"Can you get her some soup and water?" I asked quietly. I frowned at her 101-degree fever.

"Here," Decimus tossed a package of medicine toward me. She hated taking medication as much as he did, but she didn't argue this time. I immediately administered her a dose of the drug as the house came alive under the news of Vegas being sick. I wasn't surprised.

"Blue," Rocket called from the doorway.

"What's up?" I asked. I sat on the edge of the large bed and smoothed a finger over Vegas's velvet-soft lips. She was breathing deeply as she entered into a peaceful sleep. Damn, I wanted to curl up with her. I wanted to hold her so close that she absorbed right into me. She would be safe then.

"We have a hit," he murmured quietly.

My entire body froze. A dangerous smile curled onto my face. Fuck, yes. "From last night?"

He nodded. For the first time since the start of this job, I was filled with hope. I pressed a kiss to her warm head and nodded to Cosimo and Bandit.

"We're going to figure this out, beautiful," I promised softly. We would figure it out. We would figure it out, and everything would be alright. Hopefully, she wouldn't kill us for keeping something of this magnitude a secret from her.

7

VEGAS

"*I* am not missing school," I frowned. My senses told me it was approximately midnight. I faced off with Cosimo while snuggling further into Bandit's side. It probably didn't help my case that I had a higher fever than before.

"You are," he commanded softly. "It's for one day."

I let out a groan. "Kodiak is going to be in class."

"No, he won't," Bandit commented.

"I don't believe you," I scowled. "Where is everyone?"

The two of them exchanged a look that set my senses on high alert. Despite my fever, it became apparent the entire house was silent. Everyone else had left. How long had they been gone?

"They went to confront some sophomore rookie dealer," Cosimo murmured. He sat down on the side of the bed while offering me a cup of steaming tea. I took the cup with narrowed eyes. Now, why did that just seem like a whole lot of bullshit?

"What aren't you telling me? I should be there, they know that."

Bandit grumbled something incoherent as Cosimo shot him a look. I frowned further but was temporarily distracted by the orange blossom tea that exploded on my tongue. I hummed appreciatively.

"Listen," I sighed. "I may be sick, but I'm not dumb. You don't think I've realized something odd has been going on since this past summer?"

It wanted to assume the increase of Raven-related business had to do with our population increase, but I knew it was something else. There were two options in my mind, and I wasn't positive, which was the worst. Either the boys were hiding something from me regarding the Ravens, or they were seeing people and didn't want to bring their dates around. Maybe both.

"Vegas," Cosimo frowned without meeting my gaze. "There isn't anything to worry about besides our normal responsibilities."

So, it was option number two. I voiced my opinion. In my feverish state, their reactions seemed more extreme than I had expected. Cosimo's crystalline eyes went wide as his tanned complexion paled. His smooth, accented voice let out a string of fast-paced Spanish words that I assumed were curses. I had never heard him curse this much, was he upset because my assumption was correct?

"Text Blue," Bandit growled quietly toward Cosimo. I jumped at the very un-Bandit like noise he made as his arm became unmoveable around my waist. I looked up at him to find his pale green eyes darkened with anger. Why the hell was he angry?

His long pale fingers grasped my chin in a tight hold that had me frowning slightly. I heard Cosimo step out of the room while talking in a harsh low whisper. I couldn't look away from Bandit though. I was utterly entrapped in his gaze and fascinated by his odd behavior. I licked my lips self consciously, and his eyes tracked the movement with an unexpected intensity.

"Vegas," he murmured in a pained voice. "No one in this household has a girlfriend. I promise you that our increase in activity has absolutely nothing to do with women outside of this household. We haven't dated anyone since our sophomore year of high school. Why would we start now?"

My heart began beating rapidly, but I had trouble focusing on his words. None of them had dated since then? I knew they had dated in high school. So, what had changed? Hell, I knew Grover had kissed someone the other night. I was terribly confused.

"But Grover said he kissed someone the other night," I mumbled in a reasonable voice. "That was how he got a black eye."

Bandit let out a low annoyed sound in his throat. "Grover fell into a car drunk. He was just embarrassed about the reason."

My lips curled into a small smile. I was sick enough to not examine the relief my chest felt at his assurances. My arms bent around Bandit as he began to smooth out my hair. I felt his lips press to my warm forehead gently.

Still, I knew they were hiding something. At least it wasn't a secret girlfriend. I wasn't confident my heart could handle losing any of them. What did that say about me? Maybe it really was just an increase in activity, or perhaps a new part-time job? I would ask Lucida. I would figure it out. My boys couldn't hide stuff from me for long.

GROVER

I sat in my bedroom feeling like absolute shit. Bandit had told us about Vegas's confusion and conclusion about our secrecy. She was scarily observant, so of course, she had fucking noticed. Blue had underestimated her.

I had seen a lot in my twenty-something years on earth. I knew strength. I knew what made a person strong. What made someone breakable. What made someone weak. Those were the individuals you targeted. Vegas was not one of those individuals. She was the moon. A silver light of strength breaking up the darkness that threatened to absorb every single one of us.

Every time we were in a room together, I craved her eyes on me. I was selfish with her attention. I wanted all of it. She was the first and only person to make me a priority and not for any gain. No, my angel paid attention to me because I made her smile and laugh.

Before arriving in Ohio, I had lived in Chicago. Well, lived would be the wrong word. I survived. My parents were basically non-existent. They were never home. One day they hadn't come back. The only reason I hadn't died was due to Tyler. He had been a kid from down the hall and had noticed my parents' absence. His grandma, an older Polish woman, had taken me in without question. The two of us became brothers.

While attending school, the two of us had been confronted by a group of high school kids. They needed help watching some of their gang's corners. The exchange? Protection. Tyler had instantly agreed because he was worried about his grandma's safety in our neighborhood. I agreed, as well. He was family. What else was I supposed to do? Leave him alone to monitor a gang territory corner alone? Fuck, no.

The pain that coursed through my chest at the thought of Tyler's death was still fresh. We had been poorly trained to handle weapons. The kids had tossed us a pistol to keep on ourselves while on duty. They said no one would bother us. They said no one would even notice us. We were kids, after all.

Except someone did notice us. I had stepped into the corner store to grab a coke. When the gunshot echoed across the cement pavement, I knew he was dead. It had been a drive-by and fuck if I hadn't thought that it should have been me. Tyler had his grandma. Who did I have that would cry over my death? No one.

The funeral had been bare bones, and the police had quickly realized that I was essentially parentless. Despite his grandma's protests, they tossed me into the foster care system. I was pissed. I felt I was disappointing Tyler by leaving his grandma. They didn't give me a choice.

I had lost the only two people who had given me attention in my life. They had shipped me off to Ohio before I could even utter a fucking goodbye. My nightmares were still saturated with the memory of that day. Of that sound. I woke most mornings with tears on my face and a hollow feeling deep in my chest. The only thing that kept me going was my family. The family I had never expected and hadn't wanted at first.

"Screw this," I had spit out from my spot on the porch. A large house stood in front of me, and a woman named Carol stood behind me. I was trapped.

"Cut the language," a large woman demanded. She was the one in charge and seemed much younger than Tyler's grandma.

"It's going to be okay, Grover," Carol assured. "But she's right. You're only eleven, don't use language like that."

I laughed at that. Eleven? I sure as hell didn't feel eleven.

"Vi," a loud, confident voice called from the driveway. I took the distraction and turned to see three kids riding up on bicycles. The first two looked to be around my age, but I couldn't see the smaller shape behind them.

"Are these the other kids?" I sneered at Vi. I instantly had their attention. Good. I didn't appreciate it when people didn't look me in the eye.

"Blue," the red-haired kid offered me a hand. I shook it and met his gaze. He was confident like me, and I could maybe see myself being his friend.

"Grover," I drew my hand back after a cursory shake.

The other two were putting down their bikes and jogging up the drive. The boy met my gaze instantly but waited until Blue offered an introduction. "This is Bandit."

I nodded and offered him a hand. He didn't speak but did meet my hand in a firm grasp. Maybe he was just quiet?

When I moved to introduce myself to the third figure, I stopped short. It wasn't a boy. I had expected a boy, and she was 100%, not a boy. She looked up at me as she reached the top of the steps.

"Who are you?" I asked in total confusion. How was she in foster care? How could someone not want her? If she were in my family, I would have kept her. She was so small and pretty. Like the little angels in the Marshall Field's window displays downtown around Christmas.

She smiled brightly. "Vegas."

I noticed both boys hovered around her. I didn't blame them. If she were my friend, I would have been protective, too. I certainly didn't deserve a friend like her after what happened with Tyler.

"Grover," I smiled back. Apparently, that surprised Carol because she made this annoying gasp sound.

"Come on, then." Vegas grinned while grasping my larger hand in hers. "Let me show you the boys' room."

I followed blindly. I only looked back to see that both boys were watching us with careful expressions. I tried to offer them reassurance that I wouldn't do anything mean to the little angel. If I wanted to be friends with them, I would have to earn their trust. I would have to prove I would be a good friend. A better friend than I had been to Tyler. A much better friend.

"Where did you come from?" she asked with excitement.

"Chicago," I offered. My usual confidence was missing.

"Oh, exciting! That's the one with the shiny silver bean, right?"

I chuckled at that. "Yes."

"Here is your room!" She showed off the room with a twirl of her hand. It was a nice room, but I was far too enamored by the silly little angel in front of me. I frowned slightly. I wondered where she would be sleeping. If all of the boys were in here, how would she stay safe? Who was watching over her?

"Don't worry," she smiled brightly. "You will be perfectly safe with Bandit and Blue. They're family. Now, you're family too."

I nodded but didn't correct her interpretation of my frown. Instead, I followed her out of the room as my mind began to whirl. I wanted to be part of this family but knew that family didn't mean blind acceptance. I wanted to keep their attention. Her attention. I would make myself useful. I would become a fantastic friend. I would keep that smile on her face if it killed me.

I wanted to protect them like I couldn't protect Tyler. I would learn how to use those damn pistols and learn how to fight. I would make sure my family was always safe. I would make sure my little angel was always safe.

"Grover?" a sleepy voice asked from my doorway. My eyes

shot up to the door. Everything blurred from the thick tears that clouded my eyes. I saw a flash of silver as a figure collided with my chest.

"No! Grover!" Vegas whispered. "Please don't cry. Please."

I collected myself but pressed her head into my chest. She smelt like midnight rain and lilies. She felt like home. God, I loved her.

"I'm okay angel," I responded quietly. "Just thinking about Tyler."

Vegas straddled me on the bed and pressed her cheek to mine. I could feel her feverish temperature, but it didn't distract me from the feeling of her curved form against my body. I gripped her hips gently as she kissed my tears.

"We can go visit if you want," she responded. I had gone with them once to the gravesite. It was the only time I had cried in front of everyone. I slept most nights alone so that they didn't see those tears.

"Sure," I nodded, rubbing her lower back. "I would love that."

She pulled away, and despite being so sick, she looked absolutely angelic. I wanted to kiss her so badly but didn't want the first time to be when she was sick. Instead, I pressed a kiss to her forehead gently. Vegas flushed even more and traced my black eye lightly. I winced only slightly.

"Why didn't you tell me the truth?" She frowned in that cute, pouty way.

I rubbed the back of my neck lightly and blushed. "Because I'm clumsy as fuck."

She arched a brow. "And you're the guy with all the weapons? Good god."

"Hey! I'm never clumsy with weapons. Just when I'm drunk and walking." I smiled.

Her purple eyes sparkled with humor. "And when you're sober and walking."

I rolled my eyes but tucked her against me to lay down. She sighed happily and curled into my chest. I loved sleeping with Vegas. I didn't mind waking up from nightmares when she was with me. She always made my life better. Made the memories not as dark.

"How late did you get back?" she mumbled.

"Around three. About an hour ago," I responded quietly. With a nod, her breathing slowed. She fell asleep almost instantly. Tonight had been a bust. A false lead. No matter though, I had Vegas in my arms and knew she was safe and happy. Life could be much *much* worse.

DECIMUS

"Where the fuck is she?" I mumbled quietly. My cigarette was burnt out on the ashtray near her bed, and Blue slept soundly on the other side. When we had first bought the bed, I had been shocked by how huge it was. Honestly, though most beds seemed enormous in comparison to the bed I grew up with.

I walked out of our bedroom toward the stairs. I couldn't hear anything from the lower levels and assumed most of the boys had fallen asleep after our useless night adventure. Vegas's fever had returned with a vengeance yesterday, so I was more worried about her than usual. Then again, I was always worried about Vegas, even if she hated it.

I had reached a point in my life that denying her effect on me was utterly useless. She made me crazy. I fought with her a lot but only over shit that was important. I tried to make her understand why she needed to be careful, and she told me to fuck off. The female didn't realize I was trying to make sure she was safe and protected. Stubborn fucking woman.

It was also why I loved her. Well, that and a million other reasons. She didn't put up with my shit and had penetrated my heart like a bulldozer. She hadn't given me a choice. I had given her my usual shit, and she had rolled her eyes. Those beautiful fucking eyes. Shit. I was so pathetic.

I had grown up in a massive Greek family in Brooklyn. I had been the 10th kid and named Decimus because my parents were so fucking creative. Not that I ever saw my parents. No, it had been around age ten when I had started acting out for attention. I smoked every day and drank, but it didn't work. No one ever paid me any mind because there were nine other kids to focus on. We had lived in a small apartment unit that had been infested with rats and a myriad of different bugs. My only escape was school -- until it wasn't.

It had been the day before my thirteenth birthday. I had gone to school, and when I had come home, my family had been gone. Absolutely gone. They had left me. When I contacted the police with a payphone down at the corner tobacco store, they had sent a squad car down. With no other family, they had put me in foster care. Eventually, I found out my family had moved back to Greece without me. Who the fuck does that? Who just leaves their kid?

Carol had attempted conversation on our way up to the house. She seemed nice enough, but my answers were the bare-bones minimum. My family had just left me, what the fuck did she want me to say? She did let me smoke though. The woman knew how to pick her battles.

As we pulled up to the house, I caught sight of a silver set of braids. Before I knew what I was doing or why I had left the car. I had essentially jumped out of a moving vehicle with my cigarette in hand. Carol had let out a scream, but I was set on the sight in front of me.

A small girl was attempting to climb a huge tree and dangled precariously on a fragile branch. Good thing she was so fucking little, or she would have been dead.

"Get the fuck down," I demanded tightly.

The girl looked down at me and narrowed her eyes. Shit, she was pretty. Her eyes were huge, and that little mouth became pursed in annoyance. It was cute.

"No," she snarled. "If the boys can do it, so can I."

I felt my temper lighting. "I don't give a fuck what they do, you're about to break that branch and fall."

The girl paled and looked around at her situation. It really was a lose-lose. She either moved and broke the branch or waited until the branch broke. I felt panic seize my chest at the thought of her falling. So I got angrier.

"See? You're screwed."

She scoffed and sneered. "Way to be fucking helpful."

I loved the sound of her swearing. It made it easier to be mad at her. Except she somehow made it sound cute. Nevermind. I hated it.

"Jump down," I grumbled. "I'll catch you."

"No. I'm not a princess. I will be just fine."

"More like a kitten stuck in a tree."

She growled at that, and I totally imagined her as a kitten even more. I nearly laughed at the imagery but figured it would make her angrier. I didn't want her to accidentally move and break the branch.

"You're a jerk."

"Let's go, princess," I demanded. "Get down here, or I'm climbing up."

Those lilac eyes darted between the tree branch, the trunk, and myself several times. Finally, she looked at me with caution.

"Do you promise to catch me?"

I nodded.

"Fine, but if you drop me I'll punch you," she threatened.

"If I drop you, princess, you will be in the hospital."

She grumbled but shifted herself just slightly to the edge of the branch. Immediately the branch snapped, and a terrified scream came from her pink lips. She was hanging on the edge of the branch, and my arms shot out to offer her a place to land. I nodded in support as she let go. It was over within seconds.

I caught her quickly as a sigh of relief came from her. My heart instantly eased. *"See, princess? I got you."*

"I am not a princess," she stated in a beautiful wind chime tone. *"Now, put me down."*

I chuckled and adjusted her in my arms. I was holding her like an actual princess and began to tread away from the tree toward the large house. I assumed Carol would be waiting but didn't look. I was focused on the princess. That stupid cute frown appeared on her face. I loved it.

"What the hell?" a voice called out. My eyes shot to a red-haired kid.

"Blue," the girl warned. I instantly tightened my hold on her. Who the fuck were these kids? Why did she sound worried?

"Let her go," another boy growled. He was tall like me and had reddish-brown hair. I could see how upset it made him that I was holding her.

"I just saved her from a trip to the hospital, so if Princess doesn't mind, I would rather not put her down just yet," I answered quietly. My cigarette was hanging from my mouth still.

"You shouldn't smoke around her," a silver-haired kid spoke quietly.

I moved one hand, holding her easily, and tossed it away from us. He was probably right. I looked down at the princess, and she rewarded me with a smile.

"You can put me down now but thank you for saving me."
The last part was a begrudging grumble that made me smile.

"Who are you?" the taller kid asked.

"Decimus," I murmured. I expected them to laugh. It was a stupid name.

"Are you the new kid?" he asked.

"Yep."

"Well, Decimus," the red hair kid offered a hand. "My name is Blue. This is Grover."

The tall kid nodded.

"And Bandit," the ginger finished the intros.

Cool. They all had weird fucking names. I could do that.

"And my name is Vegas," the sprite grinned and hit my shoulder casually. "Not Princess."

"Sure thing, princess," I smiled.

She rolled her eyes. "Whatever, you weirdo. Come on! Let's show him his room!"

With that, the princess skipped off. I sighed, watching her as a chuckle sounded between the four of us. My eyes found the guy named Blue. "You should follow her. If you don't, she's going to be sad."

I looked up at the girl standing on the porch. She waved me over. I looked at the other boys to see if they were making fun of me. I bet they could tell I wanted to follow.

Instead, they were all looking at her with varying levels of happiness. I shrugged and jogged after her. Grover offered me a shoulder pat in passing. I guess we were cool now. Maybe this wouldn't be terrible.

"What are you doing up?" I asked Vegas. She stood in the kitchen with a large cup of tea in front of her. Those bright eyes looked sleepy, and her hair was sticking in a million different directions. In contrast to the outdated white kitchen, she was a fucking diamond.

"Getting ready for school," she smiled coyly.

"Nope," I growled. "You need to take care of yourself."

I apparently had fallen into her trap because she smiled. "As long as you promise to do the same."

"What?"

"No smoking. You're giving it up," she declared with a challenging tone. I had seen her scowling at my cigarettes often lately. Then again, the amount had increased with this new job.

I nearly chuckled but narrowed my eyes instead. Stubborn, feisty woman.

"I'll make you a deal." I sauntered forward to corner her against the counter. Her face blushed a light pink as she smirked.

"What's that?"

"If you let me call you princess, I will quit," I murmured with amusement. Her scowl became ten times more apparent.

"No," she whispered stubbornly.

"Okay, my lungs will continue their fatal path."

"Don't!" she exclaimed. "That's not funny."

"You're the one being prideful here, love," I whispered, looking at her soft pink lips.

"Fine," she ground out.

"Okay, princess," I winked. "I will pick up nicotine patches today."

"You're an idiot," she mumbled.

"Your idiot," I offered back. It caused her to meet my eyes in surprise.

"Mine?" she asked quietly. A bright pink flush colored her smooth pale skin.

"Always," I admitted softly. I had been hers since the day I had caught her from that stupidly tall tree.

"Well, then," she coughed lightly and blushed even more. "You can call me princess. But I don't want any cranky bullshit. You have to be positive about this."

"Yes, ma'am," I smirked again.

She rolled her eyes. "Are you going to come back up to bed?"

God, I loved that. I wanted her to repeat that phrase a million times and record it for my own sanity.

"I will follow you right up. I'm going to grab some tea."

Vegas pressed a kiss to my cheek and slipped past me. I watched her go. With ease, I took out my cigarettes and tossed them into the garbage. My fingers crawled across my texts to ask Booker to pick me up nicotine packets from Walgreens. He didn't respond, but I knew he would see it after his 8 a.m. class.

I was excited to be able to call my princess her rightful nickname out loud. She was my princess. She always had been. I was an asshole. I was a troublemaker. She was my soft spot. She was the sweetness that made every morning worth waking up for. She made me want to be a better man. I wanted to be a better person for her. She was the only woman to worm their way into my heart. I loved my family, but I was in love with my stubborn fucking princess.

My biological family may have left me, but now I knew what real family loyalty was like. I knew I could never leave a family like this. We all needed one another. We all needed her. It was the most uncomplicated and most complicated thing in the world.

8

COSIMO

"*W*hat are you picking up?" I asked Booker. We walked into Walgreens and made a beeline toward the pharmacy section. My eyes tracked across the many labels in both English and Spanish. The latter was still far more comfortable.

"I received a text from Deci that he needed nicotine patches," Booker smiled softly. I could tell this made him happy. I had memorized the nonverbal cues my family members displayed. It had been all I had to understand them until Vegas had aided me in becoming fluent in English.

When my parents and I migrated to America from Spain, I had been excited. When I had come home one day after school to find our entire apartment building on fire, I had been left in a state of shock. The type that only kids could truly experience. Where the first thought in your head is "No, this isn't real. It can't be."

As I stood watching the Miami fire department put out the destructive flames, a cop offered to bring me to the police station. While waiting for a social worker, I heard someone mention that the fire was the worst that year.

The social worker was immemorable, and the language barrier had been massive. I had been lucky because my school in Miami had been bilingual, so the rush to learn English hadn't been as aggressive. What I gathered from the social worker was that foster care was a fantastic system that took care of kids without parents and placed them with a new family. I didn't want a fucking new family. When a woman named Carol showed up, speaking in an elementary form of Spanish, they had told me we would be heading to Ohio. I hadn't been familiar with the state. I only knew Florida.

For most of my eighth-grade year, I was silent. The four other boys had tried to talk to me. None of them knew the exact reason for my silence, and our foster mother only spoke Russian outside of the English language. I'm sure I seemed like a total asshole to them, never responding to anything they said and not attempting to communicate. I had tried to express myself but spent most of my time studying their body language. The English program I was in at school was crap, and by the end of the year, I had grown very frustrated.

One day though, Vegas had stormed into my room with determination and changed my life. I still chuckled at the memory and wondered how long she had known the actual problem.

"Cosimo!" she exclaimed while storming into the boys' room. It had several rows of bunk beds and various gaming systems. I found the place to be very peaceful compared to school. I didn't fit in at school.

"Sí?" I asked. I had begun to understand their words but still struggled with communicating my thoughts and ideas.

"I have an idea," she smiled broadly with her hand out. For thirteen, she was small and reminded me faintly of a pixie. When I had first met her she had worn her hair in braids, now that school was over she had begun wearing it down. Blue had asked her why and she had said it was more "adult." I thought she looked beautiful either way.

I took her hand and followed her downstairs. The boys were sitting there with eager and slightly excited faces. Blue offered me a smile while Bandit slid a silver laptop toward my chair. I examined the screen.

"It's an English program so you can learn at home," Grover explained confidently.

Decimus leaned over my shoulder. "The directions are also in Spanish."

"Oh, did you know there is a different Spanish for Spain than Mexico? Well, sorta and just in some aspects," Bandit mumbled with interest. At least that was what his words sounded like to me.

"Do you like it, Cosimo?" Vegas asked eagerly and squeezed my hand.

I felt an overwhelming pull in my chest. They had gone out of their way to find a program to teach me English outside of school. Did this mean they wanted to be able to talk to me? I looked to Vegas's bright eyes. I nodded and kissed her forehead lightly. She let out a giggle. I loved that sound. I knew what that sound meant, it meant she was happy. I could work with that.

Even though I couldn't communicate with them well, they had been very accepting. I didn't fit in at school, but at home, I did. With my family, I fit in perfectly fine.

Nearly seven years later, I spoke fluent English and several other languages. I wasn't always comfortable with some humor elements of the language, and my accent was still pretty thick, but it was a hell of a lot better. Vegas had asked me every single day to practice with her until we had been able to communicate freely.

I still thanked God for putting such a confident and kind woman in my life. She always believed in me. She always encouraged me to push my boundaries. She was the reason I had gone into history at the university.

Despite my love for history, I had been told far too many times that it wasn't a lucrative or smart choice. Vegas had sat me down the summer before college and demanded I come up with better reasoning for not following my passion. I hadn't had any sound reasoning. She had made sure my major was declared and decided before stepping foot on the campus. Now in my junior year, I was the top student within my field and had received several invitations for early applications to graduate school. While flattering, I wouldn't go anywhere without my family. They were a group of people who had loved me unconditionally and made sure I fit in despite the language barrier. I would never forget that.

"You think she's still sleeping?" I wondered out loud. Booker yawned but nodded.

Once we parked, I grabbed my leather bag and jogged up the stairs. This house always reminded me of our foster home in Ohio. It was probably why we had picked it. Vegas had seen it during our house hunt, and her smile alone had sold me on the idea.

The house was peaceful. Booker's painting supplies laid untouched from the day before, and music played from the large office on the bottom floor. I assumed Blue was working on our current case. He always liked to play music while working.

At the top of the stairs, I dropped my bag and walked toward the master bedroom. My eyes instantly fell on a passed out and very sick Vegas. Her skin was flushed. Unlike

Saturday, it was a flush that told me she was ill, not turned on. I felt a shiver go through my body at the memory of our encounter that day.

"She just fell asleep," Decimus explained. He sat in her room by the window. I passed him the nicotine patches and moved toward the bed, crouching down to look at her.

"How's the fever?"

"Gone," he smiled in slight relief.

"Good," I stated. I made sure not to disturb her but adjusted the blanket slightly.

"So, is it true?"

I grinned at his hopeful tone. "Oh, for sure. You haven't noticed?"

"I'm not as good at reading people outside of seeing if they are lying," Decimus shrugged casually while putting on a patch. "You know that."

It was true. I knew Vegas's body language like my own. She was a book I had memorized. I knew every line. I knew every movement. I could tell you what she was thinking from one glance. I wouldn't tell you, but I could.

When I had caged her against the bedroom wall on Saturday, I had been playful. We had been in similar positions before, and she had played it off. This time had been different. Her large eyes had gone glossy, and those soft pink lips had opened in surprise. She had been watching my lips as we talked, and her back had arched into my chest. Everything had told me she had wanted to kiss me. I almost had. I knew I had to talk to the boys first. They had to know something had changed. It didn't stop the constant streaming of images in my head and the excitement to learn how her body responded under my touch. It would be like a new chapter to the book that was Vegas's body language.

"Something has changed," I whispered in response to his statement.

"Thank fuck," Decimus chuckled lightly. Vegas mumbled softly in her sleep before grasping my hand. Her breathing was light, and those dark lashes fluttered. I squeezed her hand in response.

"Cosimo," she smiled, faintly. "Love you."

"*Te amo*," I whispered, bringing her knuckles to my lips.

I did love her. She was everything to me. This was where I fit in. With my family.

ROCKET

I usually didn't sleep in Vegas's room. I usually slept in my shared bedroom with Booker. We were never far from one another. Tonight was different, though. I hadn't seen her smile all day, and it made me feel uncomfortable. I had asked Blue if the two of us could sleep with her tonight and he promised to tell the others. I knew it would mean Kodiak wouldn't sleep very well, but I was going to be just a tad selfish today.

"I'm glad her fever broke," Booker mumbled in a quiet voice. Out of the two of us, my adopted brother was far more talkative. I was awful with people.

I had first met Booker at a golf tournament, hosted by our fathers, in Montgomery. They were both avid golfers, and their friendship had merely progressed from there. I made a choice to become friends with Booker when I realized we were both fuck ups in our families' eyes. He was the kid with a sketch pad tucked under his arm, and I was unbearably attached to my computer games. As southern elites, the two extracurricular activities were looked down upon.

The two of us had been friends for only a month before we had been called out of school for an important announcement. At least, that was what the principal said. Unusually, our driver wasn't there to pick us up. Most kids had a mom to pick them up, but I had never met my mom and Booker didn't talk about his. This time though, our dads met us inside of a large SUV that pulled up. I paled at the memory of that day. The day everything changed for us.

"What's going on?" Booker asked boldly. I stayed quiet. I wasn't brave like Booker. My dad beat me too often to risk saying anything. I fell silent more often than not to avoid his temper. The only thing my outbursts would bring me was extensive bruising.

"We wanted to announce something very exciting to you boys," my father smiled. It was an awful smile. It promised a threat. This wasn't exciting news. This was going to change everything.

"The two of you are going to boarding school!" Booker's dad explained happily with a calculating smile.

"When?" Booker asked immediately.

"It's a military academy in Boston."

"Military?" I felt my world spin. "Why?"

"Don't worry, you will be together," my dad hissed.

My father hadn't been lying. The two of us suffered through three months of hell in a military academy outside of Boston. We were possibly the worst candidates to send to a military academy. The amount of bullying we suffered through warned us off from any healthy interactions with kids our age save one another.

Around Christmas, a woman named Carol had shown up at the academy and without explanation taken us out of the awful institution before breaking some unexpected news. Our fathers were in prison due to tax fraud. And due to our father's being assholes, we had no extended family connections. Booker didn't have a way to contact his mother even if he wanted to, which he very much did not. I had felt torn at the news we would be put into foster care. On the one hand, we were escaping a horrible environment. On the other hand, we could be trading it for a worse situation.

Booker had demanded to talk to someone, literally anyone about the situation. Carol had offered us several numbers, but they had all explained the same thing. There was no one. I knew they were telling the truth. Booker and I were really alone. So, we had gone to Ohio with Carol.

"I know you're new," Vivan explained. It was January, and the first day of high school classes following break had begun earlier that day. The other five foster kids had apparently taken the bus. She had told them to look for us at school. I wasn't sure I wanted to meet them. I really hated interacting with other people.

"Don't worry, Miss Vivian," Booker smiled. "We've got this."

"Good boys," she smiled.

The high school itself was a long gray building in the middle of an empty field. It was utterly uninspiring in every single way. I had brought my laptop for just this reason. Boredom. I knew that if I were to gain anything from this academic experience, I would have to approach the teachers regarding more advanced work.

"Come on," Booker nodded. The two of us made our way into the school and went to sign in. With a small smile, the woman had welcomed us and printed out our schedules. I knew with one glance that high school would be a dull experience.

"Shit," Booker swore. My eyes followed his gaze, and I instantly felt my heart hurt. If there was one thing I hated more than anything, it was bullying. My father had hit me around. Those boys had hit us around at the academy. Now, I was

looking at a very similar scene and had about reached my tipping point with not doing anything about it.

A smaller silver-haired boy was pressed against a locker. His face was red with straining effort. A larger boy was taunting him. A little silver-haired girl, with beautiful but enraged eyes, pulled on the big bully. I moved forward.

In the past month, I had grown bigger, and I felt more confident to handle this guy. I rationalized that I really didn't mind hurting someone if they were a bully, This guy qualified.

"Let him go," I demanded quietly. All three sets of eyes moved to me.

"Fuck off," the ugly big kid spit.

"You big ugly idiot," the little girl demanded while pounding on his back. "Get the fuck off him."

I blocked out her sweet distracting voice and moved forward quickly. After all the bullying we had endured, I had made sure to take multiple martial arts classes. I used a simple movement that allowed me to render the idiot useless. Within moments, the ugly fool laid on the floor unconscious and the silver-haired kid stood next to me gasping for air.

"Thank you so much," the kid stuttered. Booker smiled and patted his back.

"I hate bullies," the little girl growled with anger. Her eyes were on the unconscious body, and venomous rage flickered through her features. I could see a fire in her eyes. I could see actual small flames dancing a wicked pattern. I really hadn't spent any considerable amount of time around girls before, so I didn't know what to make of her. Was she normal? She seemed somehow surreal like she vibrated with something I didn't understand.

"He won't do it again," I confirmed. My voice sounded rough from not talking.

"Damn straight," she nodded before looking up and meeting my gaze. *"Thank you."*

Now that the problem was gone, I could let myself be distracted by how beautiful she was. And it was distracting. This school didn't have a uniform, and both kids were dressed down compared to the two of us. She wore a t-shirt and jeans that downplayed her radiance. At the same time, it just emphasized how natural her beauty was.

"So, are you guys the new kids?" the boy asked with a rough voice as Vegas rubbed his shoulder.

"How did you know?" Booker grinned. *"Name's Booker by the way."*

The girl smiled. "Well, you're dressed like adults for one. You also have southern accents, which is super cool. The two of us were just coming by the office to show you around."

I chuckled at that. I supposed we did look like mini-adults. I wore a polo and dress pants.

"I see," Booker nodded. *"What are your names?"*

"Bandit," the silver-haired boy smiled. He was small for being in high school, but just like the girl, he had this odd vibration of energy that seemed to surround him. Now, I was a man of science so I didn't prescribe to things I couldn't prove. With that being said, I knew damn well there were things in this universe that I didn't understand.

"Your name?" he turned to the girl.

"Vegas!" She smiled a huge grin. When she looked at me, I had to try not to flinch. I didn't want her to ask for my name. Who names their kid Reginald?

"How about you?"

"Rocket," Booker chuckled. *"It's his nickname."*

I nodded but was mildly surprised by the lie. It had been something my science teacher had coined at the academy. I was way more comfortable with it than my real name. Plus, all their names were way cooler than mine.

"Well, Booker and Rocket," she smiled. "Let's show you around."

As we began walking, she slipped her arm through mine. I didn't even realize until minutes later that I hadn't flinched. I always flinched at people touching me. Her soft voice and interesting perspective had distracted me. Shit, she was distracting as hell. Something about her small stature and sweet smiles was so comforting that I hadn't felt threatened by her touch.

No. She would never hurt me as they had. Somehow I knew that.

"She's going to want to go to school tomorrow," I noted quietly. "No way will she stay home."

I had begun to work on a program but found her light breathing and lilac scent distracting.

"No, shit," Booker chuckled softly. "She sucks at relaxing."

I yawned and put down my laptop. I was far too distracted to work. When I moved my body down on the bed, Vegas mumbled something and curled her back into my chest. Instantly, my hands were smoothing over her hip gently. I savored every soft touch we shared. It was so drastically different than anything I had ever experienced before meeting her.

"Night," Booker sounded. His head fell to the pillow, and within seconds, he was sleeping. It didn't surprise me. The guy had terrible nightmares. He always needed more sleep than he got.

My eyes shut, but my brain continued to work through our current predicament. I needed to solve our problem and figure out the puzzle that was plaguing us. That was my job. Then I would be able to focus on the mystery that was Vegas.

BOOKER

"Fucking faggot," My head slammed against the locker for the fifth time. I swore and used all my strength to push away from my attacker. This was getting so fucking old. Was our society that dense? A man couldn't find art or fashion interesting without being gay? I was officially fucking over it.

"Don't fucking touch me," I growled. My fist collided with his nose. At fifteen, I considered myself a pretty muscular kid. The military academy had gotten my ass in shape. Now, working out had become a habit, and I found myself wanting to look good for a certain silver-haired girl.

"Principal's office now," a teacher demanded. His sneer told me his bias. I rolled my eyes but strolled toward the familiar doors. Fucking Ohio. Middle of nowhere bullshit. I couldn't wait for the family to move to a large city for college. Anywhere but this bullshit.

"Booker!" Vegas commanded. She strolled into the office foyer, where I sat awaiting my fate. The principal was at lunch, so my prison sentence had to wait.

"Woman," I chuckled softly. "Do you have some type of sixth sense?"

The woman in question smiled, and my heart beat a little faster. I never considered myself a romantic, but looking at Vegas was like looking at art. Her face was perfect, symmetrical, and radiant. I never got tired of looking at her, and she moved around us with such elegance.

"I can't believe he hurt you," she murmured. Her slim form folded onto the chair next to me. She ignored my question and instead began examining my hair for blood or injuries. She was like a mother grizzly sometimes. So damn protective and cute. Her eyes were worried, and her lips scrunched up in a small scowl.

"I'm fine baby," I grinned in a relaxed voice. "He's an idiot."

"Ignore him," she demanded. "I love your art. I love going shopping with you."

She did. I knew that. I had been worried she would think my interest was odd. I had explained that art and fashion were the only connection to my mother. The one who had left me with my criminal father to marry some European movie star. Why did I want a reminder of her again?

"You're fun to dress up," I grinned happily. She was. Unfortunately, it often aggravated my other brothers. They preferred her in hoodies. They also preferred her to never interact with anyone outside of our family, so their perspective was super biased. Did she see how protective and intense we all were? Shit, man. We were just barely done with our freshman year. This could just get worse.

"Booker," the principal called.

Vegas stood up, put her hand out, and pulled me up. I stood much taller than her, but she always seemed so confident and full of life. Without argument, she led me to the principal's office. He knew to not get in her way. If she wanted to sit in a meeting with one of us, she damn well would. Anything else would and had resulted in a lot of problems. The girl was a storm, and this school was just a speck on her radar.

I knew without a doubt that Vegas would be unstoppable in life. She was inspirational. She was a muse. My muse. I wondered how long I would be able to say that. Women like Vegas didn't stay single for long.

"Booker?" That familiar wind chime voice softly tinkled. My eyes fluttered open. I instantly looked around to see that the room was bathed in the early dawn light. I had slept fantastically, which was a rare occurrence.

"You need medicine?" I asked Vegas. Her eyes were sleepy, but it looked like her fever had broken. There was a light sheen to her face that hinted to the same.

"I need a shower and some food," she laughed in that smooth and elegant way. I offered my hand to help her up.

"Do you want me to drive you to class this morning?" I asked. I didn't have my class until later on Tuesday but loved any excuse to spend time with her.

Vegas frowned, and then her eyes widened. "Oh, shit."

"What?" I asked immediately.

"I'm supposed to grab coffee with Levi," she yelped in a worried tone. "I totally fucking forgot."

Vegas started to move then. I knew the woman could move fast, but shit. She began to sprint around the room. Within seconds she had dashed into the bathroom, slamming the door, and turning on the shower. It was then that I let out a growl.

Who the fuck was Levi?

I looked down at Rocket, wishing he was up to research this guy but decided to go to the only other person who would know. I stalked out of the room and went to Kodiak's door. It was open. If I had to guess he had probably not slept well, if at all last night because he wasn't with Vegas. The man was very much a creature of habit.

"Who is Levi?" I asked point-blank. Kodiak had gone on a hike and was currently unlacing his hiking boots. Instantly, his green eyes snapped to my face and annoyance crossed those usually controlled features.

"Why?"

"Vegas is getting coffee with him," I explained. Kodiak swore and laced his boots back up.

"So?" I questioned in a slightly impatient voice.

Kodiak stood, unrolling his massive frame, and grinned with a stretch. "Levi is an asshole who is going to get smart really fast or end up very scared. He has been sniffing around our girl a little too much for my liking."

"Does she like him?" I frowned with concern and slight heartache.

Kodiak chuckled darkly. "No. He said he has a girlfriend, and he's been using the class as an excuse to get close to her."

"So, he's lied to her," I demanded.

"Yep," Kodiak smiled authentically. "So, Levi's time has come to an end."

I smiled. Kodiak would handle this. He always dealt with the guys who bothered our girl. I tried to tell myself that it would be different if she liked someone. I just wasn't confident that was true though.

9

KODIAK

*V*egas was far too nice. I could see from my spot across the coffee shop that she was feeling awkward. Her silver hair was pulled back in a loose braid, and those hypnotizing eyes were darting around the room. She felt uncomfortable *because* of Levi. I hated that.

I always knew where our girl was. Seriously. We had given her a necklace in high school, a flat Tiffany piece, that had a tracker in it. I didn't like not knowing where she was. I had told her at the time about the tracker, and she laughed. She had thought it was a joke and none of us had corrected her. It calmed my obsessive tendencies to have a fall back if she didn't answer her phone or couldn't be found.

Before Ohio, I had grown up in a large cabin in northern Michigan. My only human interaction was with my grandfather and grandmother. They both made an honest living from hunting and tracking that my birth parents had apparently looked down upon. It was for that reason that I never really understood why they had chosen to drop me off at their house and never come back. I had heard that the two of them had ended up offing themselves somewhere in New York.

When my grandparents had passed away, I had been placed in foster care. I was alone with no family. I was also fucking angry. If it hadn't been for the damned guests renting one of the properties on our land, no one would have noticed a sixteen-year-old boy fending for himself. I was surviving and doing a damn good job of it. The citizens of the small mile-long town down the road had occasionally checked on me after the funeral but trusted I could handle myself. Apparently, our property guests hadn't agreed.

When the police were contacted, I was able to keep my legal rights to the willed land but was placed into the system. It was absolute bullshit. Once I arrived in Ohio and met *them* though, I was slightly less pissed.

"Woah," the silver-haired girl chuckled. "You're like huge. Like a bear."

I smiled at her. I had been introduced to everyone, and they seemed like decent men. The woman, Vivan, appeared all right as well. If it took staying with the group of them for two years to get back my land, so be it.

Then she had walked in, and everything had fucking changed.

I had never considered myself possessive. I had always had enough to share with others. My upbringing had been filled with breathtaking beauty and solitude. So, I was alarmed by the silver-haired vixen that elicited many confusing reactions from my body at once. All of them told me that this woman was mine.

We had gathered in the living room to relax and talk before dinner. They had mentioned that Vegas, a foster girl who lived here, would arrive home soon. I hadn't paid much mind to their affectionate comments regarding her. When the door opened, and light steps sounded into the room, I turned to introduce myself.

Instantly, my eyes tracked the small women's movements. Everything about her was an absolute contradiction. She was absolutely tiny compared to me yet intensely woman. Her curves were camouflaged in boys' clothes, but her silky, curly hair waterfalled over her slight shoulders. She had a massive smile on her face and seemed to stand ten feet tall. There was a flicker of light that surrounded her that seemed nearly ethereal. If I had seen her in the middle of the forest instead of a house, I would have assumed she was a hallucination. A magical will-o'-the-wisp.

"Hey, I'm Kodiak," I offered her a hand. The bear comment really had fit. I was massive compared to her.

"Dude, your hand is the size of my head," she chuckled and pinned me with an amused look. Everyone laughed as she shook it confidently. I wasn't sure if she was always this energetic or if this was unusual. She danced on her toes. It was fucking adorable, and I did not use that term. Ever.

"Princess," Decimus casked casually, "what are you so excited about?"

She smiled and blushed. "Okay. Do you promise none of you will go all 'I'm going to kick his ass mode?'"

"Ah, fucking shit," one of them whispered barely above a breath.

"Can't promise that," Blue said quietly. The mood of the room had dipped, but if she noticed, Vegas didn't react. Instead, she smiled wider.

"Okay," she smiled widely and rose slightly on her toes. "Morris asked me out!"

The room was silent for a beat before Vivian called to her from the kitchen. Vegas smiled at me once before jogging off. No one had responded to her declaration. I felt a wash of emotions run over me. Emotions that I had no fucking right feeling.

Jealousy. Who the fuck was Morris? He apparently wasn't someone here.

Lust. She was so beautiful it hurt. Why did Morris deserve her beauty? Who was this guy?

Possessiveness. A whole lot of inner caveman bullshit going on.

"So," I asked quietly. "Who the fuck is Morris?"

Grover chuckled then with a groan. "Now, that is the fucking question, Kodiak."

"How long until dinner?" *Blue asked quietly. He had seemed like a friendly guy, but now he looked absolutely furious.*

"We have about ten," *Bandit commented quietly as his eyes darkened.*

"Stay here with Cosimo and keep them busy," *Blue instructed.* "I think we need to go chat with Morris about how this is going to go down."

"Are you coming with?" *Booker asked with a smile. I nodded and stood up. Whoever this guy was, I needed to know. I didn't like the idea of her dating anyone. Why the fuck did I feel that way? Why did I care? But my instincts have never led me astray when I had lived off the land. Why challenge them now? I followed the boys out.*

I watched Levi move closer to Vegas. Those instincts roared inside my chest. It was good that Blue was busy. I was terribly possessive, and Rocket could be as well. The worst, though? Blue. He could go from smiling to psycho in a second flat. It made me feel a little less crazy about my obsessive habits. If he was a psycho, I was, at most, a fucking stalker.

I wanted to toss her cute ass over my shoulder and march her out the door. This was bullshit. There was nothing worse than watching Vegas interact with men outside of our family. It made me physically sick most times. I didn't trust anyone with my baby girl outside of our family.

I had several good reasons not to.

Most lunch periods recently were hell. The sophomore class was small, and everyone was relatively well-known. Our family usually sat together. A few girls we had hooked up with had attempted to sit at our table. Every time Vegas had looked like she wanted to cry. Didn't stop us from dating them. But now? Now, we were fucking paying for it.

When I had first arrived, I hadn't realized the previous dating history that had occurred in our group. These fuckers fucked up. I loved my brothers, but they had been idiots. They had been hooking up with other girls from our school and a school across town. Vegas had found out, and now she felt as though she could date. It was some bullshit.

I had been with one girl in Michigan. She was the daughter of a family at our rental property. I had never seen her again. If I had met Vegas first, it wouldn't have happened. I hadn't been able to think of anyone but Vegas since meeting her. I was completely enthralled with her.

After scaring Morris, they had broken up, and she had seemed disappointed. Now, there was this new guy. She had found out what had happened to Morris and reacted poorly. The next day she had refused to sit with us at lunch and strolled in wearing a pair of painted-on jeans. My eyes had kept traveling to her perky ass, which meant that everyone else was looking as well. I didn't like that at fucking all.

"Buy her a fucking hoodie next time," I instructed Booker. Vegas had a great fucking body, and I wanted that shit to myself. Well, to ourselves. I wasn't stupid enough to ignore how everyone in the family felt about her.

Today, nearly a month later, the atmosphere was punished and pathetic. I had grown close to these men extremely quickly, and their pain killed me. Everyone felt awful. We knew she would be here soon. He was a year older than her and didn't like her sitting with us. So, she sat with him while he spent the lunch *period trying to screw her in the middle of the lunchroom. That was probably a touch overdramatic. He was just kissing her. But it sure felt like more. It didn't help she was gone most nights because he could drive. They went out to the movies a lot. Very original.*

"Screw you!" A very familiar voice screamed out from across the lunchroom.

My eyes found Vegas. Her eyes were filled with tears, her tiny frame covered in a hoodie. We hadn't seen her get home last night or arrive at school this morning. It was clear something terrible had happened. Then I saw him.

"Little girl," he jeered. "When will you fucking learn? You're only good..."

He didn't get the next horrible word out before Decimus's fist collided with his jaw. I was across the room within seconds. My arms wrapped around our girl's shaking body, and she began sobbing. I could smell the generic cologne on the hoodie and had a pretty damned good idea of what had happened. I shared a look with my brothers before strolling out of the cafeteria. Her soft sniffles and crying echoed off the empty hallways and caused a few teachers to step out of their offices in concern. I leveled them with a look, and they let me go.

We were going home. Today was fucking over. I had never been so happy about the influence being on the football team had in a small Midwestern town.

"Baby girl," I whispered soothingly. My hand smoothed over her wild hair as I unlocked our large minivan. I didn't even bother putting her in the passenger seat. I kept her on my lap and began driving home. Not before I pulled off that fucking hoodie and gave her mine. It seemed to soothe her, and I tried to not overthink how much I liked her smelling like me instead of that asshole.

"Kodiak," she whispered. "I'm such an idiot."

"Vegas," I pleaded softly against her ear. "Don't cry. You won't ever have to see that piece of shit again."

In fact, I hoped my brothers would remove his ability to fucking see. He didn't deserve her memory. He didn't deserve anything, except to be dropped in the local river for police to find. Or not. No one would miss him. I could guarantee it.

"I wanted to call you guys this morning, but I was so embarrassed," she frowned as we pulled into our cul-de-sac to park. "I thought he loved me."

"Hey," I whispered, grasping her chin softly. "You don't need his love Vegas. He's a worthless piece of shit who didn't deserve you. If he did, he would have been on his knees, worshipping you. Don't ever forget how fucking amazing you are. But, baby? No matter what has happened, what you have done...you always fucking call me. I just want you safe and happy. I was worried about you last night. You never stay out for the night, and it scared the shit out of me. I'm going to put a fucking tracker on you or I will lose my head."

I was rambling, which was unusual for me.

She took a shaky breath and nuzzled into my neck. "Okay. You're right."

"Come on," I whispered, picking her up and trying to ignore my reaction to her lips so near my neck. "We're going to go take a nap and watch some Netflix."

Later, I would be sure to emphasize how upset I was that she didn't call and maybe figure out that tracker thing.

As we watched movies and held her, I texted the boys. We needed to have a talk later. Vegas wouldn't be dating any of these losers and neither would we. We were a family, and she was our girl. I would prefer to share her with these eight lunatics than ever have her look outside of our family. Screw those bastards. They didn't know her. She was ours. She was mine. No one would take her away from us.

Since then, her dating experience had been limited and that aspect had been mostly of her choosing. I had been there for each date and every moment in between. She had yet to bring it up, but I knew she saw me. I hoped she felt safer knowing I was there. The house always fell into chaos when she went on a date. Even now, my phone buzzed with update requests.

I didn't take my eyes off her.

Levi touched her cheek, and I lost it. He shouldn't touch our girl like that. I was up and across the room in seconds. The pretense was over, Cosimo had said she was ready. If she weren't, this would be revealing my cards. Oh, fucking well.

I had never claimed I was a patient man.

VEGAS

I had woken up feeling rejuvenated. While I felt guilty about missing class on Monday, the boys had been right. Now I was not only feeling better but far more well-rested. I drank my coffee while entertaining Levi's thoughts on our class. I told myself I only had to sit here for another half-hour. Another half-hour of ignoring his odd compliments. Hadn't he mentioned a girlfriend?

Levi wasn't ugly. He had dark wavy hair that hung around his ears. His eyes were a light brown surrounded by thick lashes. His face was angular and classically handsome. If it weren't for his ugly personality, then I might have considered dating him.

As it was though, he was awful. He had a very negative disposition and complained about everything. It made for dull conversation. Add in some creepy compliments, and you've got an awkward morning coffee date.

Oh, shit. This was a date.

"How's your girlfriend?" I interrupted.

His eyebrow shot up before he smiled. He reached across to brush the hair from my cheek "Ah, no worries, Vegas. We broke up actually."

There it was.

"Get your fucking hand off her," a smooth, husky voice demanded. I almost smiled. Kodiak was my little date stalker. I loved him for it.

Levi frowned but retracted his hand. "Who the fuck are you?"

Levi was a big guy, but Kodiak was huge. He stood behind my chair and lightly touched my shoulders. He was my armor and shield. His shadow extended over me and covered Levi's form. I wasn't usually one to take pleasure from others' unease, but Levi had lied to me about having a girlfriend. I was now positive about it.

"Her boyfriend, so fuck off," he demanded. My heart jumped at his words. Was he serious? Was he actually staking a claim? Shit. This could get messy.

"You're dating him? But I asked you to coffee!" Levi yelled with frustration. Okay, this was dramatic. My face turned pink as the room quieted. It didn't help that the Ravens drew attention without trying simply because of our reputation and somewhat secretive life. Add in a little drama and it was like roadkill. You couldn't take your eyes away.

"Raise your voice at her again and see what happens," another voice purred dangerously low. Blue appeared behind Levi. I was momentarily distracted by the leather jacket he wore. I was also distracted by the tone of his voice. I wasn't obtuse. I knew Blue wasn't always the dimpled cutie that called me beautiful. I just wasn't usually around when he went all "scary motherfucker" mode.

"Who are *you*?" Levi shot back. I noticed his bag was in his hand as he stood. His questions were stupid because I was damn positive he knew precisely who Blue and Kodiak were.

Everyone watched. The coffee shop had become a silent vacuum. I worried about the tension building. Something had to explode, right?

Blue's lips tilted into a dangerous smile. "Her boyfriend. Now, fuck off."

Levi cursed and stalked off. I instantly relaxed but ignored the obvious elephant in the room. How was I dating both of them? Ha! Wouldn't that be nice? Then I wouldn't even need to deal with the drama of possibly ruining my family's well-constructed balance.

Instantly, Blue smiled. "Good morning!"

Kodiak chuckled and grabbed a seat. "Take your time next round. I could have gotten a hit in."

"Nope," Blue smiled at him and then looked at me. "Now, beautiful, we have to talk."

I nodded. I was beyond confused.

"Do you like Levi? We want you to be happy, but you looked uncomfortable," Kodiak asked quietly.

"I thought he had a girlfriend," I explained quietly. People were still staring at us.

Blue sighed. "He lied."

I shook my head. "No, I don't like him."

Kodiak grinned. "Good, because your boyfriends would be super jealous and shit."

"My boyfriends?"

Blue chuckled. "Beautiful! The two of us just announced we were both dating you to an entire coffee shop. Don't break our hearts."

I rolled my eyes. "Let me guess. I conveniently have eight boyfriends?"

Kodiak exchanged a look with a pleased Blue. "Well, I am sure they would want to officially ask, but at least you're in the spirit of it now."

"Funny guys," I teased back. "This is why I never date. You guys are too scary."

"Oops, sorry," Blue dimple grinned. He wasn't sorry.

"None of those guys deserves you," Kodiak reasoned with sincere puppy dog eyes.

I laughed softly. "Alright, you two, my new boyfriends have to walk me to class."

"Absolutely," Kodiak smiled, offering a hand. Blue stood up and walked in front of us backward.

"Everyone out of the way!" he announced in a mock announcer voice. "The most amazing, perfect, beautiful girl-friend ever needs to get to her class!"

I flushed bright red as the coffee shop broke out in laugh-ter. The crisp autumn air felt fantastic on my searing face as Blue stepped into stride with us. I barely noticed when he took my other hand. They had been joking about dating, right? Why was I okay with it not being a joke? I mean, the looks were a little odd. At the same time, they were no different from the usual looks we received. When I was between Kodiak and Blue, I felt beautiful. Screw everyone else.

Man, I was really living in dreamland over here.

"What classes do you two have?" I asked curiously.

"Nonverbal communication," Blue explained lightly. Blue was a communications major, but his focus was primarily on business models.

"Marine biology," Kodiak responded in a huff. It hadn't surprised me when Kodiak had decided to become an environmental biology major. However, the man was a delicious pine-smelling survivalist that had been relatively upset with having to take a water-based course. He was more of the camping-in-the-woods type of guy.

"What about you?"

"Criminal psychology," I chirped happily. It had been an easy decision to become a psychology major. It only made sense with how observant I was, and if I was honest with you, the classes came easy.

"Wait up!" a familiar voice called out. We turned to see Booker and Rocket running to catch up to us. I briefly noted that both looked disheveled and I took the time to look over my boys, feeling as though something was slightly off.

Blue looked freshly showered this morning. His red hair was styled neatly, and those bright blue eyes seemed electric against his black leather jacket and jeans. On this left hand, he wore two rings, one of which was on his ring finger. His tattoo, a simple black outlined heart, was underneath it. I had asked him about it once, and he had told me that his heart would belong to whoever he married, so why not tattoo it there? I had loved his response. I had also tried to ignore my insane jealousy at the thought of Blue marrying anyone besides me.

But it would happen, right? I couldn't keep all of them. They weren't Pokémon. They were real boys. I tried to ignore the glaring Pinocchio references in my head.

Kodiak smelled of fresh pine but wore clothing that looked lived in. If I knew him, he had come home from his morning hike and jogged off to stalk my date before changing. He had always been my little stalker. I had never brought it up to him because I felt safer with him nearby. He was like a massive grizzly bear. His dark, chestnut hair was messy this morning, and those dark green eyes bright behind his glasses. He made me want to curl up and cuddle.

"Is that...blood?" I asked with sudden panic. My steps brought me to Rocket. His multi-colored hair was messy, and those grey eyes seemed tight. His body was rigid, but his hands softened to grip my hips. I began to inspect the collar of his light blue polo.

"Biology class," he offered. I frowned at him. I knew he had been in the biology lab this morning, but that didn't explain the blood. Did he think I would believe that? Or was he offering something in an attempt to distract me? I ran through his pre-med schedule in my head before determining that he may have been telling the truth about the class.

Booker grumbled a warning. "Rocket."

"That was where we came from," he explained quietly. Clearly, my face expressed my confusion, mistrust, and potential hurt.

"Shit, I can't do this," Booker swore and looked away. My gaze fell on the sleeve of his paint-splattered jeans and button-down. His dark blonde hair was pulled into a bun, and his ears glinted with small sapphire earrings. The only thing that stood out? The blood that stained his shirt sleeve.

Then it clicked. I twirled on my toes and looked directly at Blue.

"Will Levi be in class, Blue?" I asked quietly in a dark tone. "Or will he be at his apartment icing his face?"

Blue's jaw tightened as those eyes darkened to navy. "Probably the latter."

"Are you fucking serious?" I stepped toward him with vicious intent before an arm wrapped tightly around my waist. I instantly smelt sea salt and knew it was Decimus.

"He yelled at you," Grover explained quietly.

"Have you thought about how awful the class will be for me? How awkward it will be?" I broke away from his grasp and turned to face the two of them. My finger jabbed into Grover's muscular chest. "No, you fucking didn't, did you?"

Of course, both of them looked far too handsome for the morning. They were dressed in athletic wear, and both held a post-workout shake. It was clear they had just finished an early morning sparring session. Grover's auburn hair was sweaty, and Decimus's fair skin was slightly flushed. How the hell did they look good after working out? I always, without exception, looked like a drowned, sweaty rat or tomato. Then again, they were both in the athletic training department, so it made sense that they were used to it.

"Come on, princess," Decimus whispered softly. "He was a total ass."

"No," I growled sharply. It was moments like this that I needed my two pacifists.

As if summoned from above, the two missing members made their way over. Cosimo wore an oversized hoodie that had the flag of Spain printed on it. His hair was styled sharply and glinted like the silver lip ring he wore. Bandit wore his signature oversized shirt and black gauges. If I had to guess, the two of them had been headed toward their mid-morning class. Cosimo in the history department and Bandit in the English department. I couldn't let them distract me though. The added beauty of their presence made me irrationally angry.

How dare they look so good when I am trying to make a point! They beat up a man for raising his voice at me. How was that okay? Then again, he really shouldn't have raised his voice at me. But, shit. They should have at least asked if I wanted his face black and blue. It was only polite.

Shit. I was sorta messed up, wasn't I?

"You can't jump every single guy who says something to me that you don't like," I turned an admonishing gaze to Blue and Kodiak. I knew the power dynamic in our group. I knew who had made this call.

"Negative, darling," he drawled with a slow smile. "That is something I have and will continue to do."

"Fuck this," I growled out while walking away. "I'm just going to stop telling you who I go see!" All of them seemed to offer different but similar looks of unease. Good.

"Oh, that's right!" I called out with a dry chuckle. "Kodiak will just track me, so it doesn't really matter, does it?!" I was further away now.

"Oh," I pointed at the two of them. "And by the way, I'm breaking up with you two. You're no longer my pretend boyfriends!"

I stalked away. Not before Blue raised his voice with audible frustration. "It wasn't pretend, beautiful."

I rolled my eyes. *Always fucking joking about something.* The doors to my class building were heavy. I yanked them open and came face to chest with a hard solid chest that smelled like a smoky bonfire and copper.

"Fuck," I snarled.

"Woah," a deep smooth voice laughed. "Put the claws away, kitten."

My eyes shot up and further narrowed. It was B.

God, I hated The Letters. I assumed, upon my first meeting, that they had terribly massive egos or awful first names. One of those two options had been correct. A and K were terribly annoying individuals, but they had nothing on B. This guy had always been a piece of overconfident and egotistical work.

"Don't touch me," I moved past him. He was a big guy. His skin was that even, rich kid tan from too much time out on his boat. His teeth were so bright it hurt to look at them. He had shiny, pale blonde hair and dark brown eyes. If it weren't for everything about his personality, I would say he was extremely handsome.

The door to the building shut and he tugged on my hand. I hadn't gotten very far before I turned to glare at him. "What did I just say about touching me?"

B smiled. "Come on, Vegas. I didn't mean anything by it."

"It wasn't what you said," I stated quietly. "'It's just you."

He chuckled, shaking his head, as something that looked oddly like frustration and hurt filled his gaze. "Those boys have brainwashed you, doll."

I felt rage bubble up under my skin. I stepped closer. While I stood two steps above him, we were close in height. "Yeah, B? Let me guess, you're not the egotistical bastard they accuse you of being?"

B's smile grew. "No. I am 100% that."

"Then what do you mean?" I asked with reservation and slight confusion. B opened his mouth to respond before narrowing his gaze behind my shoulder. I knew without looking who had arrived. The scent of Fireball permeated the air as Blue let out a low dark chuckle.

"Go on B," he goaded near my ear. "Tell her about your theory."

The Letter's face grew pink with embarrassment and frustration. He sighed. "Never fucking mind. Vegas come find me when you grow tired of their overcontrolling bullshit."

I didn't respond to his statement. My eyes narrowed on his retreating form. I had a feeling that some of my boys would be outside. I turned to look at Blue and give him a piece of my mind.

Except instead of meeting his beautiful blue eyes, my lips pressed against his.

Oh, shit.

I should have stepped back. I should have apologized. I hadn't known how close he had been standing. I hadn't known his soft lips would be in kissing proximity. I didn't pull back, though. For a moment we were suspended before his body tensed and my hand gripped his wrist for stability. Those soft overwhelming lips pressed further into mine and I gave in. A low, sexy sound vibrated through his muscular chest.

"Fuck," I whispered. Our lips melded together again in an all-consuming kiss. I couldn't think. I couldn't breathe. I could only feel. Blue's strong arms swept me into a vise hold against the stairwell wall. My hands trembled against his jaw as they locked his face to mine. I needed his kiss like I needed air.

It was rough. His hips pinned me to the wall in a possessive lock. It was hot. My entire body felt ignited as if there had been an explosion in the center of my chest. I was entranced by his deep, passionate kisses. How had I missed out on this for so long? How had I survived without this?

"You are ours," Blue purred with dangerous tension. His entire body and voice spoke to a level of possession I had never experienced. "Not B's. Not the Letters'. Not Levi's. Ours. Tell me you are ours, Vegas."

I forgot my anger. I forgot my previous doubts. I only heard the command in his voice. I had to answer it. It was a compulsion that ran up my spine and extended throughout my entire body like a virus.

"Yours," I whispered softly with a tiny nod. He hummed appreciatively and deepened our kiss once more. My head began to spin from a lack of oxygen, but who needed air, *right?*

A cough interrupted our tongue fucking. By the way, *yes* -- that is exactly how hot it was. I pulled back to look at Blue's sparkling eyes and his small wicked smile. What had I done? What the hell did this mean? What had I unleashed by admitting to being theirs? What the hell did he mean by it? Oh, dear lord, here comes the anxiety.

"Hunny," Lucida sighed from the top of the stairwell looking amused and slightly shocked. "You have an audience."

Blue didn't move from our position, but I took a moment to look away from his face. Fuck. The class bell had rung. How had I missed an entire class period? The whole stairwell was frozen with students staring at us. This included a bruised Levi, half the Letters, and all of my boys. The only group of people who didn't look upset? My boys and Lucida. She seemed to think this was very funny.

"You bastard," I whispered softly. Blue chuckled and stepped back from pinning me to the wall. He turned toward the stairwell and nodded to Deci.

"What the fuck are all of you doing here? Get out!" Decimus smiled a wicked wide grin as people jumped. The students began to scramble out of the hallway. The Letters stood their ground for a moment before disappearing as well. Any drama regarding the Ravens would no doubt make the social rounds within the hour.

"Well, well," Lucida teased. "Little Miss Class Ditcher."

I rolled my eyes but looked back to Blue. He stood with his eyes locked on my face in a way that made me feel hungry. I missed his touch already but had no idea how to ask for what I wanted. I wasn't even positive where we stood.

"Forgive me?" he whispered softly. I could hear the other

guys laughing and talking around us. None of them seemed to think our actions were unusual. What did that mean? Did they not have feelings for me like that? Why did that hurt? Shit, what the fuck is wrong with me?

"Maybe," I huffed before stalking off. He chuckled but let me go. Lucida smiled and hooked arms with me while humming a happy tune. I may have looked back down at my boys once more before leaving for my next class.

All of them looked back at my retreating form. What I hadn't expected to see? Desire...and not just from Blue. What the heck?

10

BLUE

*I*f being around Vegas without touching her hadn't been difficult enough before, it would now be impossible. I would be walking around with a perpetual hard-on. That kiss had been everything. It had been a perfect coincidence that class had let out in time for everyone to see me staking my claim. Let the fucking Letters look. Let Levi look. Vegas was ours, and she was going to realize what that meant very soon. I heard her speak the words but had listened to the confusion behind them. I was done with not touching her. I was done with not kissing her. I needed her like a drug, and I wasn't exactly known for making rational choices as it was. Those soft lips just encouraged me to work harder to finish this case. The sooner it was over, the sooner we could make plans for the rest of our lives.

Make no mistake, that was *precisely* where this was headed.

"I want tabs being kept on Levi and the Letters. More so than usual," I explained to my brothers. We walked toward the parking lot. I could tell all of them were hyped up, and no one denied the reason. I had opened a floodgate and risked rejection. When she had kissed me back, Vegas had permanently sealed her fate, so I hoped our girl was ready for this. For us. She had said she was ours, but the reality of that could be overwhelming. We weren't exactly a very easy-going group.

Then again, maybe Grover was right, and I wasn't giving her enough credit. The woman continued to happily put up with us most of her life. She had chosen us time and time again, so it was time to tell her that we had chosen her...a really fucking long time ago.

"Listen up," I commanded. "Vegas said she was ours. That does not mean we go overwhelming her."

"So, no mauling her in the hallway?" Decimus goaded. He had an unlit cigarette between his lips and a nicotine patch on his arm. Had he decided to quit?

"I didn't say that," I grinned. "Technically, she kissed me. Let her take the lead."

"If she starts getting too confused, she will panic," Bandit commented softly.

"If at any point, even in class, you see her freaking out, get her little ass home so we can explain what the hell is going on. I am hoping she will come to the conclusion on her own, but if not, I would rather we explain then for her to feel guilty."

Everyone nodded their consent.

"We've got a problem," Rocket grinned as his eyes darkened. My phone buzzed. I heard the buzz of everyone else's phone as well. That was very unusual.

"Motherfuckers," Kodiak growled.

I felt every protective bone in my body go still. The text had been sent to eight contacts. It contained a photo of Vegas. She was sitting in class with her right shoulder toward the camera. Her eyes were trained on the teacher. Whoever had taken the picture had been walking past her classroom.

She's mine. Hands off or she disappears. Only warning.

The world exploded into motion. I commanded without thought. Rocket began tracking the number. He would go with Grover and Kodiak to pull Vegas from class. I sent Booker and Decimus onto campus. They would put out feelers from their contacts. Who wanted our girl? Who would be brave enough to threaten us?

"Let's get the car," I murmured. Bandit and Cosimo followed me to the parking lot.

I needed to see our girl, and I was putting our family on lockdown for the night.

VEGAS

My eyes closed with exhaustion. I loved psychology, but this morning had exhausted me, and my teacher's voice was ringing in my ears. Blue's kiss was the only sensation I could feel anymore. I prayed this class would end sooner rather than later. I was turned on and anxious as hell.

"Vegas?" the teacher called from the front of the room. I could feel eyes on me. My eyes snapped open as a figure appeared in the door.

"Yes?"

"It seems the Dean of Students would like to speak to you." Ms. Groves held a neatly printed pink appointment sheet. I nodded before standing and blushed as everyone stared at me. That reaction, of course, made me scowl because I don't fucking blush ever. Blue had me all messed up.

The student who held the slip was familiar. Maybe a

seller? No, that didn't seem right. He didn't look like the drug type at all. I immediately categorized his features. He had high cheekbones and smooth pale skin. A pair of soft blue eyes rested under dark brows and short black hair. The young man offered me a faint, promising smile. I felt my body tense at that, and all of my instincts were telling me this guy was off.

"I will email you the PowerPoint," Ms. Groves assured me. I smiled and followed the young man out. He was a head taller than me and dressed in expensive, business casual clothing. Was he a student or a faculty member?

"What does the Dean need to see me for?" I asked curiously.

The boy shrugged. "No idea. I'm just a student worker."

"Cool," I nodded as we turned towards the stairs in awkward silence.

"You're Vegas, right?" he asked, curiously. His eyes seemed cautious and jaw tight. Suddenly, the soft blue eyes from class iced over, like frozen water. I could feel the shift in his entire body. Why in the heck did it feel like he was mad at me?

"Yeah," I nodded cautiously. "And you are?"

We pushed out of the department doors. He didn't have an opportunity to answer before he flew back into the stairs. My mouth popped open in surprise as a curse tumbled out. Kodiak was on him instantly. His hand locked onto his throat as Grover wrestled a phone from the man's grasp. What the literal fuck?

"Rocket?" I whispered in a horrifyingly small voice. He wrapped a protective arm around my shoulder and brought me in tightly to his chest. He offered me a phone. His phone. I almost dropped it. The text on his screen was disturbing.

Who had taken that picture? I instantly looked at the

now unconscious young man on the stairs. Grover tossed the phone to Rocket. He momentarily scrolled through the phone before recording some elements inside his own. He shook his head and threw it back. Grover slipped it into the man's pocket and stepped away.

"We're going home. Now." Kodiak demanded. His eyes were filled with fury and fear. Rocket let me go as Kodiak picked me up like a doll. I wrapped my arms around his neck and encouraged him to tighten his arms wrapped around my upper thighs. I had no intention of arguing. I couldn't get over that text just yet. It was disturbing and uncomfortable.

"Call Blue and explain," Rocket ordered Grover. He was on the phone in an instant. I thought I heard yelling, but my exhaustion was back with a vengeance. The adrenaline was not being kind to my recently ill body.

"Sleep, baby," Kodiak encouraged with a far softer voice than before. "We are going to handle this. I promise. I won't leave your side."

His permission was what I needed. My eyes fluttered shut for a moment. We were home when I woke. My yawn made Kodiak smile softly, but the smile didn't reach his eyes. No, he was still agitated.

"Where is everyone?" I whispered. We were in my bedroom and the early afternoon sun lit up the entire room in hues of silver and white.

"Looking into our little problem," he whispered with tense posture. I was spread out in the middle of my bed as he sat on the edge. His hands were threaded through his dark hair, and his glasses were tossed to the side.

"Kodiak," I spoke quietly. "Come to bed."

His dark green eyes flashed with low burning heat. With slow movements, he unlaced his boots and shrugged off his jacket. In mere seconds, Kodiak had crawled onto the bed and maneuvered his large frame in between my hips. Instead of resting his head on my stomach, he had caged me. My nose was inches from his own. I couldn't escape the intensity of his gaze.

"I'm safe," I whispered. "Really, Kodi. Everything is fine."

"It won't be fine until I know who they are," he growled softly. Something dark flashed in his eyes. Something like anger, but different. Darker.

"Why?" he whispered in a pained voice.

"Why, what?" I murmured. My hands caught his face gently and made gentle patterns on his skin.

"Why did you walk out with him?" I caught my sarcastic retort before it left my lips. I knew he wasn't blaming me. I knew he was terrified. I could see the fear of losing me burning underneath his anger. I tried to respond honestly.

"He said the Dean needed to see me and he had an official slip," I explained.

Kodiak sighed but nodded. "I know. I'm not blaming you, baby."

I tried to not look into it too much when he called me baby because it wasn't very often. Although, it had increased lately.

I hated the tension in his face. I hated the anger and fear. I moved swiftly to flip us. Only because he let me, my hips locked down on his in a straddle. A deep rumble echoed through his massive chest. I swiftly grasped his massive paws and pressed them to the pillows on either side of his head.

"Vegas, I almost lost it when I saw that text," he whispered through a rough low voice filled with pain. The sun broke through my bedroom windows and cast a stunning pattern across his left cheek. Those dark green eyes seemed to sparkle with gold. I could have called him beautiful, but that still didn't seem like the right word for Kodiak.

"Don't worry, I'm safe. I promise. I'm right here, and nothing happened to me." I spoke with my lips close to his ear, causing a shiver to roll through his body. Suddenly, a hardening presence under my hips became far more noticeable.

"Promise me," he demanded. "Promise me you will be so damned careful from now on. I would lose my goddamn mind if you were taken."

"I don't think I have an option but to be careful," I responded. "You all will probably be following me every-where from now on."

"Damn right," he murmured. His hand broke from my grasp and reached for my neck. Those large fingers grasped the delicate silver necklace I wore around my neck. It was the one piece of jewelry I never took off and the way he touched it made me feel like it was far more than just a necklace.

"Never take this off," he commanded with a penetrating gaze. "Do you understand me?"

"It really has a tracker in it?" I whispered with wide eyes. Did I want to know the answer? How crazy was too crazy? How intense was too intense? Before he even said anything, I had decided that it didn't matter because part of me had known that Kodiak was a tad obsessive. His deep worried gaze grew determined as he nodded. I think he expected me to get pissed. I think he was gearing up for a fight. I didn't have one in me. I was still freaked out.

Later? Later I may punch him for being such an over-controlling bastard. Not now, though.

"Okay," I conceded.

"Don't be scared," he pleaded softly. I was terrified, and it the only reason I didn't fight him on the tracker. God forbid I was kidnapped. It could save my life. Honestly, it was pretty fucking smart, but I would never admit to that.

"I just need to know who took that photo, you know? How did I not notice someone snapping a photo of me?" I swallowed hard.

"This is not your fault, Vegas. We will get this creep before you can blink," he promised.

I blinked.

He chuckled and pulled me closer. His large arms clasped my waist tightly as we rolled over once more. I stretched out underneath him as his body moved against my own and his chocolate hair brushed against the bottom hem of my shirt.

I let out a giggle at the tickling sensation. A goddamn giggle. What the fuck was wrong with me? Giggles were reserved for watching cheesy vampire movies and swoon-worthy love scenes at sleepovers. I was very disappointed in myself.

He grinned viciously and caught my shirt in his teeth. I felt my entire body still at the imagery of his massive body between my legs. His brilliantly white teeth were clasped around my thin shirt as he peeled it away from my bare stomach. All right. Not disappointed in myself. I'd fucking giggle anytime for this.

"Don't look at me like that," he growled softly. I breathed with rapid intensity as he continued to gaze into my heated face.

"Like what?" I whispered. My voice sounded low and husky, a far cry from usual.

He chuckled while resting his chin against my soft stomach. This felt very different. Something had changed. I would know since Kodiak had been sleeping wrapped around me for all of college. My toes curled, and hips opened to allow for his massive frame. A deep rumble vibrated through every nerve of my body.

"Like you're hungry baby girl," he murmured. His sculpted lips pressed a soft kiss to my stomach. My eyelids fluttered shut in response. Fuck. My stomach exploded in butterflies that began a slow warming sensation.

"Maybe I am," I whispered before blushing. His answering growl was enough to encourage my hands that easily sunk into his thick dark hair as he pressed another warming kiss to my skin. A quiet, satisfied sound escaped my throat. It caused Kodiak to groan.

"I wonder," he murmured quietly.

"Wonder what?" His kisses trailed across my cleavage to the base of my neck. I felt my head fall back in surrender. My entire neck was exposed to him and his soft kisses. Something he seemed to like if the constant rumbling in his chest told me anything.

"I wonder if all of you tastes as sweet as your honey skin," he rumbled softly.

"Oh, shit!"

Kodiak let out a deep frustrated chuckle as my eyes moved to the door. Booker stood with wide eyes and a goofy grin on his face. He didn't look apologetic in the least. Fuck! Had the door been wide open this entire time?

"Dude," Kodiak chuckled.

"Sorry," Booker grinned again. "Although, this probably won't be the last time."

"Fair," he nodded. "It's going to be an interesting dynamic."

"What the hell are you two talking about?" Both of them looked at me with matching stupid grins.

"Nothing, baby girl," Kodiak offered me an innocent look.

Booker rolled his eyes. "Come downstairs to see my finished painting."

He was gone and my gaze fell back to the massive man on top of me. I shook my head and began wiggling out from under him. His gaze was playful and empty of the worry or anger from before. I loved it. I tried to not overthink this situation. What if Booker told Blue we had been kissing? Well, we hadn't kissed, but it probably looked like we had. Would Blue be mad? What would Kodiak say?

"Stop," Kodiak commanded.

"Stop..."

My question was cut off by a sweet honey-filled kiss. My body went limp with pleasure. His lips were smooth and soft against my own. Holy fuck! His tongue pressed gently into my mouth and sweetness exploded in my mouth. It was like sucking on a sugar cube. A soft moan emerged from my throat. He pulled back just as quickly as when he had started the kiss.

"Alright, get your cute ass downstairs." He swatted my butt playfully.

"What?" I was dazed, and my eyebrows were fixed in a confused expression. I feared it was permanent. He chuckled and carried me towards the door. In seconds we were downstairs and in the completed living room.

"Oh, wow!" I exclaimed authentically. The sugar on my lips reminded me of Kodiak, but my confusion and quiet panic were gone. Booker's murals always did that.

"You like?" He wiggled his eyebrows.

"I love!"

I really did. The entire room was a pale purple. The feature wall, where our grey couch sat, was highlighted in a bright gold pattern. Upon further inspection, it was clear that the entire shape created a brilliant raven silhouette. The wingspan was massive and tilted on an abstract angle. While everything was drawn in an outline, there were a few select feathers on each wing painted in metallic gold. Ten to be exact. It was amazing.

"You are an amazing artist, Booker," I whispered appreciatively.

"I just have a fantastic muse," he offered me a flirty wink. What the heck? When did he start winking?! I felt my face flush pink. I knew Kodiak had seen his wink, what did he think?

My phone buzzed briefly. Before I could grab it, I felt it slip from my jeans. I rolled my eyes but let Kodiak check it out while I examined the mural further.

"Are you fucking joking?" Kodiak swore.

I turned as my phone jumped in the air toward Booker. Kodiak was up the stairs with impossibly fast movements as Booker met my eyes. His gaze was terrified and furious. He motioned for my migration across the room. He held up the phone screen.

I warned them.

I felt bile in the back of my throat. Everything began to blur at the image in front of my face and accompanying the text. What the actual fuck?

"How?"

It was a picture of Kodiak and me in bed. My head was tilted back and filled with amusement. It was the moment he had tickled my stomach with his soft lips. It had been a private fucking moment. A moment that someone had been watching. I felt rage boil through my system as my hands began to tremble. Fury. I was fucking furious right now.

"Call Blue! Right. The. Fuck. Now!" Kodiak yelled down

the stairs. I glanced at Booker as he dialed. My feet moved toward the stairs as I stepped up silently. Kodiak was swearing. I knew something had happened upstairs, something to make him curse like that.

"Oh, wow," I whispered with undisguised horror.

I could see my master bedroom from the staircase but continued to move forward towards the doorway. Kodiak's gaze met mine, and every ounce of happiness from earlier had bled out to be replaced by fury. The screen window, which had been opened for fresh air, had been cut straight down the middle. The entire section of flooring that stretched from the window to my closet was drenched in blood.

Raven blood.

Dead ravens.

They were piled together and bleeding fresh, dark blood. At least twenty of them. Their little bodies were so freshly dead, they almost still had a fucking heartbeat. I watched the blood slide from the pile of birds toward my sock covered feet. Kodiak moved toward me with caution.

"Vegas," he soothed. "We're going to go downstairs, okay?"

The blood was red. It seemed black though. Blood couldn't be black, right? Or maybe it was blue. That seemed right. Blood was blue. This clearly wasn't blood.

"What is she doing?" Another voice asked quietly. Booker?

"I don't want to move her," Kodiak murmured. "She's about half a moment away from a full-blown panic attack. Think freshman year times ten."

Was I about to have a panic attack? Was he right? I drew my arms close to hold my waist as I swayed back from the blood onto my heels. It moved far too fast. It touched my white sock.

"No," I whimpered. No? What was I saying no to?

"Get her the fuck off the floor! Now!" A hard cold voice demanded sharply. So sharp. Whose voice was that? No one attempted to move me.

The blood fused to my sock and at some point, my knees broke. Booker spoke in low tones as other voices joined his. I was shaking so bad my teeth chattered. I could only see the river of blood that poured toward me and covered the feet of my very loud boys. Why were they so loud? Why were they fighting? Why did the blood seem so much thicker than before? How was there so much? The bodies had to bleed out eventually, right?

"Don't touch her," Kodiak snarled.

"She's covered in fucking blood!" A voice roared. Decimus?

"Freshman year." He spits out before my hearing became static again.

Freshman year? Oh yeah, the panic attack of freshman year. That was bad. I had been triggered. Her death had caused me to be irrationally uncomfortable with a few choice situations. Freshman year had included one of those and I had been brought to the point of an extreme panic attack. The boys had tried to move me from my spot frozen against the wall, and I had gone absolutely bat shit. I had torn into Kodiak's chest with my nails. He still had small scars.

Was this situation that bad? The blood continued to turn my jeans black. I felt my eyes flicker and roll back as the room went dark.

"Fuck. Make the water warmer," Someone commanded. I laid against a hot chest. Whose chest was this? I liked this chest. A lot.

"She has blood everywhere," another voice mumbled. My clothes were peeled off with ease until I could feel only the soft cotton of my boy shorts and bra. The shower spray blasted against my skin. We were in the shower. Why? I had taken a shower this morning.

I felt long, cold fingers start to massage my hair and scalp. The scent of pine surrounded me. Before I got a grasp of my surroundings, the water disappeared, and my body was wrapped in a thick cotton towel.

At some point, I blacked out.

COSIMO

"Everything about this situation is fucked," I snarled to Bandit. My arms were locked around Vegas's unconscious figure. Her trademark silver locks were wet and tangled. Poorly scrubbed blood crusted her towel-covered form. Her cotton bra straps were soaked and a faint pink color. We had moved her downstairs for now. I worried she would grow cold, though, so I made sure to tuck a blanket around her slight form.

"You think?" Bandit responded dryly.

Blue was furious. His commands echoed through the house. It was moments amid the chaos that I was thrilled with my position in our family. Bandit and I weren't fighters. Both of us had a temperament best suited to calm others down. It was particularly useful when it came to Vegas and her panic attacks. My specialized skills, historical and linguistic knowledge, were as useless as his thieving ability in this situation.

"We need to get this place secure," Blue snapped before stepping into the room. His eyes focused entirely on Vegas. Both Bandit and I adjusted ourselves to offer him room. He knelt down in front of her to adjust the sizeable fuzzy blanket cocooning her.

I saw any semblance of sanity disappear from Blue's eyes. It was like a rubber band snapping. They hardened in determination as he pressed a soft kiss to her forehead. I could see the singular focus reaching an all-consuming point for him. Vegas mumbled something quietly before her eyes fluttered open.

"Shit!" She scrunched her nose in pain. I found my hand moving to her temple, and I began smoothing out the pressure point with gentle ministrations.

"Vegas," Blue commanded her attention.

"Blue," she responded faintly in a distant tone.

Suddenly, her attention was sharp and focused like a razor. I watched her thoughts connect rapidly as the past hour came flooding back. Those sparkling eyes became harder than even Blue's unhinged gaze. Honestly. The two of them scared me. I loved them both, but they both had their own special brand of madness.

In a quick movement, Vegas sat up straight. She looked down at her towel and blanket-covered form. After a small frown and shake of her head, she commanded our attention.

"I want this fucker gone," she whispered in a heated voice. "Tonight."

"We are working on it."

Vegas stood up with a smooth move that seemed preternaturally graceful. I stood with her as Blue mirrored her action. He seemed to be waiting for something.

"I want to try to draw him out. Tonight," she demanded softly. "I am going to go get ready. We are going to our usual Tuesday spot."

"Vegas," Bandit whispered. His voice was low and hollow.

"No," she growled softly, her entire body shaking with anger. "This is happening."

"Use my bathroom, not your bedroom," I offered.

Blue spoke then. "I am not okay with this, Vegas."

Vegas stepped forward into his space, chest to chest. "I am doing this, Blue. I want it done, and I want it done tonight. I am not living in fear. Not after what happened to her."

I knew immediately of whom Vegas spoke. Blue paled as his eyes sparkled with that hidden madness. He nodded in consent. I led her away from the living room. As we reached the stairs, I quickly picked her up. She grumbled but easily locked her legs around my slim hips. I was able to keep her gaze averted from the macabre scene that was her bedroom. Most of my brothers were attempting to clean as we passed.

"How long until they figure out the plan for tonight?" she whispered against my neck. I locked my bedroom door and showed her to the shared bathroom that connected to Grover's room. A screaming match began downstairs.

"I would say now," I chuckled. Decimus started to curse in Greek around a minute later. Vegas shook her head before turning on the shower. I forced myself to offer her space but didn't leave my bedroom. It was far enough.

A knock sounded on the door.

"I have clothes and makeup for her," Booker explained over the sound of the continued screaming. I opened the bedroom door and offered Booker a nod in understanding. He stepped into the bedroom with a relieved sigh. I knew how uncomfortable yelling made him. If I had to guess, Rocket would soon follow. It wasn't that they were opposed to fighting and arguing, but yelling matches seemed to really bother them.

"How is she?" he asked in a low voice.

I looked to the partially closed bathroom door. A billow of steam from the shower poured into the bedroom as her voice rose in a light, airy hymn. She seemed fine.

"I have no idea," I admitted honestly.

Booker put a hand on my shoulder in a comforting way. "Just keep an eye on her. You will be able to tell if she starts panicking."

I would. Right now, though, she seemed fine. That worried me. How could she be okay?

Another knock sounded on the door. Booker let Rocket and Bandit in. All four of us shared a tense look. Downstairs the more temperamental half of our brotherhood exploded in a new round of screaming. Clearly, a divide had become apparent. The one voice I didn't hear? Blue's. That was bad.

Suddenly, the bathroom door opened.

My heart stopped somewhere between my throat and mouth. Vegas stood with an amused smirk in the bathroom doorway. Her slim curved frame was wrapped in a small towel that showcased her mile-long legs. Everything about her looked revitalized. She truly was okay.

"Close those mouths," she chuckled, grabbing her clothes. "It's not like you've never seen me in a towel before."

No one said a word as she closed the bathroom door.

"Hiding out was a fantastic idea," Bandit whispered. Rocket chuckled as Booker shook his head in amusement. I agreed. *She was wrong though.*

It was different. So much different now.

VEGAS

"*B*oys!" I yelled over their raised voices.

I stood in the living room archway with as much poise as I could manage. Panic attacks always had the habit of exhausting me. I tried to ignore the painfully bright memory of blood painting my master bedroom floor. The panic had no place here. The blood was gone. We needed to figure this out.

"You're not leaving the fucking house," Decimus snarled. I briefly noticed the nicotine patch on his arm. Good boy.

"Why?"

Well, that silenced them. Bandit lounged behind me with a carefully placed expression. His long fingers massaged my lower back in comfort as Cosimo held my hand. The dual support was much appreciated.

"What do you mean by 'why'?" Kodiak asked with sincere confusion.

"Why can't I leave the house?"

"You have a fucking stalker!" Grover exploded as his eyes flashed dangerously. It took me off guard because Grover usually was calming Decimus down, not getting worked up. He was yelling, which meant that he was very worked up about this. I felt terrible that this situation had brought him to this point.

Blue sat silently. I knew he understood my point. It was probably the only thing he consciously understood right now. He looked unhinged. I couldn't imagine what this situation was doing to him. He was a bit of a control freak.

"A stalker who left dead birds in my bedroom," I stated with malice boiling under my skin. "A stalker who took pictures of Kodiak and me in bed, without us noticing. A stalker who was able to retrieve numbers for all of our secured lines. I don't know about you three, but I don't think it really fucking matters if I am in our house, at school, or at a bar. So, you can stay home if you want, but I am not about to sit around terrified of my own shadow. It's not happening."

Silence.

Decimus let out a string of curses before turning towards the kitchen. Grover walked out of the front door with a perfect scowl etched into his handsome face. Freakin' drama queen. Kodiak groaned and fell into the couch beneath him. The tension in the room had been broken.

Blue met my eyes and stood. I was unfamiliar with this Blue. He was the Blue that I rarely saw and only sometimes heard about. Everything about him screamed danger. Those bright baby blues had turned navy sparked with madness. It was hot. Although also slightly scary to have all that intensity focused solely on me.

"Everyone out except Vegas," he demanded softly. In all my time with these boys, I had never seen a room clear out so fucking fast. Traitors.

Blue backed me up against the wall with practiced predatory steps. If it were anyone besides Blue, I would have been terrified. Instead, a hot lash of desire uncurled in my abdomen. His forehead pressed to mine as he began speaking in low even tones. It took a solid second for my brain to catch up to his words. I was distracted by the way his large warm hands held my waist and how the scent of cinnamon tickled my nose.

"You will stay with someone at all times tonight, Vegas. You will not leave my visual space for even a fucking moment. If you need to use the washroom, you better fucking bet someone is going to stand outside the stall. I am not playing around with this, do you understand?"

"I get it, Blue."

"No," he growled primally. "I'm not sure you do. Someone wants to take you away from us, Vegas. From me. Someone is threatening to make you disappear."

A dark shiver flooded my body.

When his left hand captured my chin and forced my attention, I felt a small pathetic whimper escape my throat. His eyes, usually a bright sky blue, were painted a deep navy with fear and anger. The words that came from his mouth next were sinister enough to set my hair on edge.

"And full disclosure, beautiful? When I find him. Yes. *When* not if. I will kill him."

"Blue," I offered in a strangled voice. It wasn't that I didn't believe him. I did believe him. I felt like his promise was only the start of a change overtaking my family. It scared the crap out of me, and I felt as though I was always trying to play catch up.

"Now," he grinned viciously. "Let's go handle some shitty drug dealers."

The change on his face was instantaneous. The unhinged look in his eyes remained, but those damn dimples made an appearance. So cute. Cute enough that I may have temporarily forgotten his grave death threat.

"All right," I sighed with confusion.

"Good girl," he purred. His hand tilted my jaw more as he stepped into my space fully. My heart began rapidly beating at the feel of his muscular chest against mine. My eyes trailed down to his perfect lips. He waited. I knew he wanted me to make the first move. *So I did.*

My arms wrapped around his neck securely as my lips molded to his in a heated kiss. A satisfied groan escaped his throat and swallowed up my whimper. His kisses tasted like ecstasy and fire. A flame lit up my entire nervous system in one sweep. How could a kiss taste this fucking good?

"My beautiful Vegas," he whispered in a coo. "You've got this entire fucking house wrapped around your finger."

"What?" I whimpered as his pelvis ground into mine in a rhythmic motion. His hands pinned my wrists to the wall in an unbreakable hold. Those lips hovered above my own in a magnetic embrace.

"Tell me," he whispered. "Do Kodiak and I taste different?"

Oh, shit. My face flamed red as he continued a careful assault of kisses against my throat and jawline. Was he mad? He didn't seem mad. I clearly meant mad as in angry, not unstable. He was very clearly fucking insane. *And I loved it.*

"Answer my question, Vegas."

"Yes," I whispered.

Blue made an appreciative noise from the back of his throat and continued to press me further into the wall.

"I would bet," he whispered, "that we *all* taste different."

All? Oh, sweet Christ.

"Vegas," a voice sounded from the doorway. "Oh, shit, sorry."

I heard Cosimo but couldn't look away from Blue. He wouldn't allow it if I tried.

"How do you think he tastes?" Blue's voice was smooth, but his eyes were lit with a challenge. Did he want me to kiss him? What in the everloving hell was going on here? Cosimo stepped into our space and leaned against the wall. It effectively caged me between the two of them and left little room for escape. Not that I wanted to escape.

"Do you want a taste, Vegas?" Cosimo asked with genuine curiosity. His crystalline eyes were lit in excitement, and those sculpted lips worried his silver lip ring. Did I want to kiss Cosimo?

Fuck, yes.

"Come on then," Blue encouraged, nipping my ear. "Take what you want, Vegas." Had I nodded my consent? I must have.

Blue let go of my wrists as Cosimo stepped into my space and peered down at me. His rich cologne reminded me of leather and sandalwood. He brought both large palms to my cheeks and ran a singular thumb across my lips. Due to his height, I balanced on my toes to reach those perfect lips.

Apparently, I took too long. The minute I moved forward, Cosimo took control of our kiss. His arms wrapped around my waist in a vice hold that molded me to his chest. My feet left the ground as his tongue licked the seam between our passionate kiss. Blue had been right, this kiss was different. His taste was different.

I had never seen Cosimo as an impatient individual, but that was his kiss. It was impatient and demanding. It was devouring and overwhelming. I could feel my vision blur as everything grew dizzy with pleasure. He kissed the life out of me. It was as if he had waited his entire life to kiss me and would now devour every part of my mouth in a deep, hungry kiss.

"Holy shit," I exhaled. My eyes bore into his as Cosimo let out a shaky breath.

"It seems the rest of our family is eager to leave for the bar, shall we?" Blue asked in amusement. My eyes snapped to his as the foyer grew loud with boisterous voices.

"What the hell is going on?" I mumbled with authentic confusion.

Blue grinned down at me. Cosimo had placed my feet on the floor but kept a warm hand on my lower back. "I told you Vegas, you're *our* girl."

Blue strolled out of the room before offering any other explanation. My eyes met Cosimo's gaze. Amusement and adoration filled those crystalline eyes. Was he serious? I thought he had meant "*our* girl" metaphorically. Had he not? He couldn't... I mean that was unreasonable... selfish even. They were my boys, but I couldn't be their girl...right?

"Let's go, beautiful!" Blue's voice sounded from the foyer. Cosimo tugged my hand and led me toward the door. No one batted so much as an eyelash at my swollen lips and loose braids. My confusion continued to grow.

"Let me grab a jacket," I mumbled. My steps took me toward the coat closet as the boys began walking toward the car. I caught sight of myself in the large foyer mirror and raised my brows.

I looked, well...loved. I unbraided my long hair and examined the delicate pink blush that filled my cheeks. My eyes held a glossy, exciting look to them, and my lips were soft and red. Shit. I looked fantastic.

I ignored my hidden panic and shrugged on my long black trench. Booker had chosen a pair of leather high waisted pants and matching thigh-high velvet black boots. My slender upper body was wrapped in a long sleeve black top that showcased very little skin. Somehow the look was sexy without being obnoxious. I nodded in approval before meeting Bandit at the door.

"You're okay?" he asked quietly. I looked up at him and found myself once again surprised by his height. This was the same kid who was bullied in high school, right?

"Yes," I murmured softly. He nodded and took my hand in a firm grasp. The two of us locked up our house and walked toward the large SUV. I briefly wondered what Blue thought of me holding hands with Bandit. Did Cosimo care? Would Kodiak be upset? Why did it feel like everyone knew something I didn't? Shit. I needed to talk to Lucida.

Once we were situated in the car, I zoned out. The car ride was peaceful, but my body could only cope with so much at a time. I attempted to compartmentalize the array of dramatic events that had arisen today. Was it possible I was dreaming? Maybe I had gotten so sick that I was hallucinating? Either that or I had fallen down the rabbit hole. How else had everything changed so much within a day?

"Who is on our list tonight?" I asked quietly. Our car pulled into the parking lot with ease as we found a space near the front. Somehow, a spot was always open there. My guess? The owner had purposefully left it reserved. Bar and club owners as a whole tended to prefer our presence to the police.

"Some regular," Rocket sighed. "His product has been reported to be laced."

Rocket managed our online database. It was a forum that allowed students to submit anonymous tips. He always had a list of possible problem groups. Specifically, we had been having a lot of tips being offered about The Letters. Unfortunately, the claims were far too broad in range for a confrontation.

Six of Clubs, unlike the club Stools, was a typical college bar. The shape of the bar was square in nature and consisted of dark red brick walls surrounded by tall shrubs. The door was scuffed from far too many drunk idiots falling into it or kicking it open. The pavement was littered with cigarette buds and empty bottles. It was a place visited by all and loved by none.

"Ah! My favorite girl," a booming voice chuckled. A grin spread across my face as I caught sight of my only real friend outside the Ravens.

"Nathan!" I sprinted forward to collide with my massive friend.

He let out a booming chuckle that had the crowded bar pausing for just a moment. The sound of AC/DC hammered my eardrums as the scent of beer blocked Nathan's warm, whiskey scent. I pulled back from the hug to smile up at my friend.

"How have you been?" I asked with keen interest. Nathan had inherited Six of Clubs from his deadbeat dad. He had attempted to make some changes but found each one was met with adverse reactions. People liked their shitty college bars.

"Good," he smiled with those pearly teeth. "Busy though."

"Same," I nodded, feeling like a bobblehead. I went to speak, but Nathan's sudden stillness had me turning toward the door.

I knew his reaction wasn't due to my boys. While they

hadn't befriended Nathan like me, they were tolerant. Most of them offered nods of greeting and occasionally stopped to talk with him. I wondered what they saw in Nathan that made him an exception to their norm of isolation.

"Fucking great," Nathan sighed. His large hand racked through his bright blue hair in frustration. I watched as The Letters, all of the boys at least, made their way into the establishment. Their tightly fitted blazer and polo ensemble seemed at odds with the establishment vibe.

Kodiak stepped in front of me and completed the wall of boys that had assembled. My hand found Nathan's elbow as the large man let out a grumble. He knew the drill but had explained how being protected by a college group made him feel like shit. The Letters had pull on campus though. *Power*. They could have his bar shut down.

"No need to hide your little gang princess back there," K goaded with a smile. "We're just here to relax and enjoy the appealing environment."

A chuckled. "Don't look so tense, boys. Not everything is a war."

Except it was, and I didn't trust their assurances one fucking bit. B met my gaze, those warm brown eyes burning into my skin, as he offered me a look that I didn't understand. It seemed to be one he shared with Blue as well in passing. Then the group of nearly nine men made their way to the back of the bar. A set of vinyl booths sat back there. They claimed all of them.

"Listen, Nathan," Blue spoke in a quiet tone his eyes still on B. "How much security do you have on staff tonight?"

"Two of my fraternity brothers are showing up in about an hour, why?"

"That should work. We are going to help with security

tonight. I don't trust their reason for showing up tonight. No offense, but they would never be seen here."

Nathan chuckled. "No, shit."

"Can you keep Vegas up front at the bar with you?"

"Hey!" I scoffed while nudging Blue's shoulder. "I'm right fucking here."

He wiggled his brows. "Don't I know it, beautiful, but until the other threat is handled, I don't want you alone."

"Threat?" Nathan looked curious His amber eyes melted into a shade of honey-like Decimus.

"No," I growled. "I've got enough overbearing protective..."

"Stalker," Kodiak interrupted. "She has a fucking stalker. Now, go on to the bar and sit your pretty ass down."

Nathan immediately grabbed my hand and tugged me toward the bar. I pouted but didn't express my discontent. I had won a battle by forcing them to leave the house. I knew arguing for more freedom right now would be a bad idea. They were an intense, overbearing bunch. It wouldn't take much for them to snap and just say "fuck it" and leave the state. I am not joking about that. Kodiak has mentioned several times going to his Michigan estate.

"So," Nathan grumbled. "Tell me about this stalker, Vegas."

I rolled my eyes but accepted the freshly poured beer he pushed my way. The man knew the way to my little black heart. Quality beer. *Shit.* Maybe I did hang with the boys too much. Lucida was always saying that I acted more like a boy than a girl. I wasn't sure how I felt about that.

"Just some tiny prick dick who gets himself off on scaring me," I mumbled. My nervous tic, running a hand through my mass of hair, made an appearance. Nathan would flip if he knew.

"Understatement of the fucking century," Booker stated quietly. I bit my lip nervously and peered over at him. Tonight he wore his dark blonde locks loose and straight. His white, high neck coat was loose around his muscular form and complimented his beautiful gray eyes. He looked very much the male model tonight and seemed to glow inside the dark, dank bar. If I wasn't terrified of sounding cheesy, I would say he looked like an actual angel.

"Explain," Nathan demanded. He worked to fix a drink for a woman down the bar before returning. I scowled at Booker. Booker royally ignored me and began to explain what had occurred since this morning. Holy fuck. That had been this morning. Also, I had kissed three different men in one day.

Oh, my. Blue *had* opened a floodgate.

Suddenly, my panic bubbled up in true Vegas fashion. I blinked away tears from the onslaught of memories. This morning I had been annoyed with Levi. He had made our coffee meeting a date, without asking. Now, I had a stalker. A creepy, picture-taking, bird-killing stalker. Shit.

"Vegas," Booker whispered. His hands were wrapped around my shoulders as he attempted to make eye contact. I blinked away the tears as he offered me a concerned expression.

"I'm fine," I mumbled. Nathan made a frustrated sound before placing a hand on my arm in comfort. I let their support console me. They would keep me safe.

Who would keep them safe? What if the stalker hurt them?

"Vegas," a sharp voice demanded.

My eyes shot up to Decimus. He stood with burning, honey-colored eyes filled with a heady cocktail of under-standing and frustration. I took the hand he offered and followed him toward the narrow hallway near the left side of the bar. The minute we turned the corner, I was enveloped in a rib squeezing hug.

"Princess," he murmured softly against my ear. "We can leave right now if you want to. Just say the word."

I let out a shaky breath and tried to compose myself. Decimus always had this effect on me. His strength made me stronger. His boldness made me bold. His presence was a powerful wave that crashed over my very being and washed away any impending weakness. My exhales became steadily stronger as I maintained eye contact with his silky blue shirt.

"No," I swallowed my panic. "I've got this."

His chest rumbled as he tilted my head back gently. "Promise me. If at any point you feel like going home…"

"I'll be sure to tell you."

With a slow exhale, he nodded. "All right. Let's go handle this dumbass."

"He's here already?"

"Walked in right before I saw you freaking out."

I brushed off my pants and straightened my spine. His eyes shone with soft pride as he took my hand in his and led me toward the bar.

I could do this. I was strong.

DECIMUS

I observed her expressions as we made our way toward the alley entrance. Nathan allowed us to use the alley for these types of things. Half of our crew stayed inside to watch The Letters as I took Vegas toward the rest. Bandit, Blue, and Cosimo were already there. The tall, lanky figure, our target, stood against the wall with a look of anguish on his features.

"You? Really?" Her windchime voice drew the attention of our problematic user.

"Vegas," he greeted quietly.

"So, I'm guessing there was no meeting with the dean today?" she laughed derisively. Her voice took on that icy quality I hated. It was sharp and filled with disgust.

Blue tilted his head with consideration as the other two backed up. She stepped forward into the man's space and sneered. To his credit, those blue eyes never moved from her gaze.

"No, there wasn't," he snarled back. All at once, a sense of fear and premonition exploded within my chest. This was all wrong. He was far too calm. He had targeted her earlier for a reason, and now she was inches from him. I had the overwhelming urge to pull her back behind me. My hands twitched as I met Blue's sharp gaze. He could feel it, too.

"You knew your product was bad?" she asked with thickening disgust.

"I laced it purposefully," he mumbled with angry hooded eyes. The surprise must have been apparent on my face because Blue shook his head. I knew this guy was lying. If it was only that simple. If he was our problem, we could grab him and end all of this in one sweep.

"Do you make a habit of sampling your laced products as well?"

"I'm not high," he growled.

"Liar," she spat out.

I saw it then. I saw what she saw. His skin was pale, a sickly color like rotten fruit, and his eyes were so dilated they were nearly black. He vibrated with an unusual amount of energy, nearly manic, as he kept his focus locked on Vegas. I immediately felt my senses awaken in response to a threat aimed at our silver-haired princess.

"Beautiful," Blue murmured. "Step back from him."

I knew his words would have an adverse effect. I just didn't realize the extent of that effect. I heard the sharp click of a safety being turned off as Vegas instinctively stilled.

A gun.

The motherfucker had a gun aimed directly into her lower abdomen. My stomach lurched, but I didn't dare move. Time itself seemed to stop. I couldn't see a way out of this.

Vegas let out a laugh that sent ice down my spine and turned Cosimo's face white. Bandit's eyes filled with undisguised dark intent mimicked by the four of us. Rightly so.

"You're going to kill me?" she purred quietly. Her hands were trembling, but the rest of her was perfectly poised.

The man frowned. "I have to."

Vegas raised a hand from her waist to his pale skin. He flinched but allowed her soft touch. He seemed nearly soothed by it. Fucked up fucker.

"Who?"

The man shook his head before his eyes darted toward the bar door. It was enough for Blue. In one movement, he knocked the gun onto the alley pavement before moving between the two of them. Vegas tripped back into Bandit's hold as Cosimo reached for the gun. My foot landed a well-placed hit to the back of the man's knees that brought him crashing to the ground.

"Grab Rocket's medical supplies, now," Blue demanded. His eyes locked onto the man as Cosimo tossed me the gun and jogged inside.

"What is he on?" Vegas snarled.

Blue began to search his pocket but found nothing. Not even a wallet. He hadn't expected to walk away from this.

His breathing was irregular, and those translucent eyelids flickered before closing.

Rocket was out of the backdoor in seconds, his small briefcase opened to reveal an irregular amount of syringes. He took a blood sample from the unconscious man before administering him something in a nondescript vial.

"What was that?"

"Drop him at the front of the building. Nathan called an ambulance. We can't kill him. They will know it's us."

Blue shouted demands as the unconscious body was dragged toward the front of the bar. We cleared the alley and moved toward the parking lot. Vegas was silent the entire time. I was the only one to notice it besides Bandit. The two of us shared a concerned look before squeezing her slight frame between ours.

Our problem had gotten larger. Local dealers were sampling the dangerous product being spread around. Now, it seemed The Letters had ordered a hit out on Vegas. That would need to be handled. She could have died. Hell, she almost had. *Fuck.* This was all fucked up. My heart and head hurt at the idea of ever losing our princess. I would rather die.

At least we would be able to test the product now that we had a blood sample. That was a small blessing. My hand closed around Vegas's pale long fingers. Her gaze was filled with an indiscernible expression. Guilt, possibly? Why the hell did she feel guilty?

BLUE

My vision blurred black. I could feel it seeping in from every corner, whispering for me to find him. To kill him. I knew I had to. I had to know he was dead. He tried to kill Vegas. He

131

didn't deserve to be alive. Neither did The Letters. We would handle them later.

"I'm coming with," Bandit spoke in a low, calm tone. He sat in the passenger seat after the car emptied. I had stayed behind. Decimus had carried Vegas into the house, sparing me only a glance of understanding before taking her inside. Rocket dropped his bag into the house before returning with a different color case. I knew the others would take care of Vegas for the time being. I also knew the others would feel some semblance of guilt for killing him.

I wouldn't, though. Bandit wouldn't. Rocket wouldn't.

The drive to the hospital was quiet. It was near midnight. The autumn air was filled with the scent of bonfire smoke and sea salt. I usually would have appreciated such a beautiful night. Today, I didn't have it in me to care.

I had killed for Vegas once already.

After her death, the one that had nearly sent Vegas spiraling to a place from which we almost didn't get her back, the police had taken the man into custody. Unfortunately for him, that wasn't good enough for me. He had tried to hurt Vegas, too. He had wanted to touch her. I did the one thing that would ensure that would never happen. I killed him. The same two men had been with me that day. It had never surprised me that Bandit and Rocket were a little dark on the inside. I wish I had justifiable reasons in my past as they did. Instead, I had accepted the fact that I was mentally unstable when it came to my woman. It had been that incident that had cemented it.

All it had taken was slipping into the town's small jailhouse at night. A picked lock and cyanide tablet. It looked like a suicide case. It was anything but that. Vegas never knew, and she wouldn't know now unless she asked.

"How can I help you, gentlemen?"

"We're here to see our friend. He was just admitted for an OD," Bandit mumbled. His large green eyes widened at the woman. The local hospital was small but sufficient. Clean, yet homey. Much too trusting.

"Of course, poor kid," she sighed.

In moments, we stood by his bedside. Alexander Kadence. Levi's older brother. The two of them were a pair of want-to-be Letters. Now, one of them would die. Maybe the other if he didn't stay away from Vegas.

"I'll give you boys a moment," she mumbled before leaving us alone.

"Cameras?" Bandit asked quietly.

"Checked the system. We are good to go," Rocket assured. He opened his silver bag and handed me a slim syringe.

"What is it?"

Rocket offered me a wicked smile. "Just administer it."

I trusted the good doctor but hoped this would kill Alex. I wanted him dead. From the look in Rocket's eyes, I had a feeling he did as well. I found a place on Alex's neck, hidden under his shirt, as if they had missed it – and pushed.

"We have five minutes," Rocket mumbled.

The three of us left the room. No cameras. No official sign-in. Far too much trust. It would appear as if he had died of a drug overdose.

"Please call us with updates," Bandit pleaded. He slipped a silver card toward the woman at the front desk. She nodded.

As we exited the small hospital, a code was announced overhead. My smile grew as I imagined the call we would be receiving tonight. Luckily, it was on a secure line so the police would find it routed to another state if suspicion arose. It was also why we had worn hoodies for the lobby cameras.

I felt the blackness recede as contentment came over me. No one would hurt Vegas. *Ever.* Now to deal with The Letters and unknown stalker.

VEGAS

"Yes," I mumbled on the phone. "I am perfectly fine, Nathan. Just a bit of a scare."

He grumbled something over the noise of the bar. "You would tell me if you weren't?"

"No," I grinned. "But I really am fine."

"Okay," he sighed. "Goodnight, Vegas."

"Night," I mumbled. My phone clicked off as I leaned back into the tub. My eyes fluttered shut as guilt flooded my chest. *I could have gotten my boys shot.* No longer was my stalker the only threat. No. Now The Letters, if my hunch was correct, wanted me dead. I knew that the accidental death of any other Ravens would merely be an added benefit in their eyes. They were fucked up like that.

Guilt seeped into my skin. I didn't even care that I could have died. It was better me than them. What if it had been them? What if he had placed the gun into Blue's stomach or Decimus's head?

With a pained groan, my head fell forward into my lap. The master bathroom was a beautiful mix of blue and green tiles that showcased an impressively large claw bathtub.

After being nearly shot, I had found it oddly easy to be back in my bedroom. Skewed perspective, right?

"Vegas?" A soothing voice called from the door.

"Come in," I shouted back.

"Really?" Bandit asked with honest surprise.

"Bubbles," I chuckled. My body truly was covered in bubbles, excluding my long silver hair that was piled on top of my head. The entire room smelled like lavender and mint. I couldn't have been trying harder to relax. Literally. It *was not* possible.

"Oh, wow," Bandit laughed. "Are you stressed?"

I eyed his teasing tone. "Where did you get that idea from?"

He smiled and pulled the vanity chair next to the tub rim. I tilted my head to the side and examined his face. There was a lightness to it that hadn't been there an hour ago. Then it clicked.

"Where did the three of you go?"

Bandit's face tensed as those spring green eyes connected with my own. "Do you really want to know?"

Did I? I wasn't kidding myself, I knew where they had gone. I had stopped being able to blame unexpected deaths on luck since *he* died in our small-town jail cell. Shit like that seemed to happen a lot to people around me. Specifically, people who hurt me. It was how the guy who had stolen my virginity had ended up in the hospital with destroyed ribs and shattered wrist. Goodbye football career.

At first, I felt guilty that I didn't feel more awful about it. Then I considered my position on it. How would I have felt if someone had hurt my boys? Enraged? Yes. Murderous? Yes. Guilty? H-E-double-hockey-sticks no.

"No," I sighed before leaning back into the tub.

Still, guilt flooded back with a vengeance as my eyes

watered, but guilt motivated by something else entirely. Bandit made a low pained sound in the back of his throat before moving off the chair to kneel at eye level.

"Vegas, he was..."

"No," I sniffed and grabbed his hand. "This isn't about him. I could have gotten you killed. I could have lost any of you in a second."

Bandit let out another pained sound and unlaced his shoes with graceful movements. I watched him peel off his shirt, leaving his pants, before stepping into the tub. My eyes widened in surprise. It wasn't that Bandit was shy with physicality. Not in the least. But the move was far bolder than I expected. Bandit didn't look embarrassed in the least. Instead, he stepped into the water. It spilled over onto the tile. He didn't care. He reached for me as his long limbs slid down on the other side of the circular tub. I climbed forward completely unabashed by my nudity.

This was Bandit. I had known him for nearly twelve years.

I reached my arms around his neck as he carefully placed his large palms on my hips. Tears still trailed down my flushed face as his spring green gaze memorized my expression. I set my forehead against his own and embraced the comfort he offered. This was why I loved Bandit.

"Please don't feel guilty," he murmured quietly. "Please."

"If I had lost any of you," I whispered tersely. "I couldn't... I wouldn't be able to..."

I think that was when I started crying in earnest. I hiccuped and felt tears slip down my cheeks while clinging to his half-naked form in a bubble-filled tub. If it weren't for my heavy guilt, I would have laughed. Bandit probably would have as well. Instead, he hummed a quiet tune and smoothed a hand down my spine.

A soothing calm saturated my bones while I laid in his arms. I could feel his steady heartbeat beneath my head and the sound of his even breathing. I clutched him tighter and heard a small groan escape his lips.

"What's wrong?" I asked, looking up into his darkened green gaze. Those eyes were hooded with unabashed desire that caused my entire body to straighten in response. There was something so confident and relaxed about Bandit. He hadn't always been like this. Now his shirtless, tattooed chest, laid bare as his lips crooked in a knowing smile.

I turned my attention to those tattoos. The artwork created a carefully constructed fantasy world. Each mythological creature represented a family member. My hand traced the small fairy he had claimed was mine. He let out a low hiss at my touch and gripped my hips in a bruising hold. My hands decided to move on their own accord to grip Bandit's silky hair. His nostrils flared in response as my eyes flickered to his lips.

"Kiss me," I demanded softly. "Please."

Bandit let another tortured sound escape before he surrendered to what we both knew was inevitable. My lips skimmed his in the barest of touches before the scent of fresh grass and vanilla seeped through my nose. I nipped his mouth gently, nearly playful, as he tilted his legs, so my body slid forward. My bare breasts pressed against his colorful chest as my greedy lips moved against his own. I could feel every part of his bare skin against my own and the sensation was overwhelming. It felt like he had plunged us into an electric current while underwater. Electrifying and exciting. My lips craved his touch, the longer we explored one another.

I pulled back gently to look into his sculpted face to softly whisper his name. A bright pink flush invaded his skin as he offered up another electric kiss. I moved my body against his own to create some type of friction beneath the water.

"I love you, Vegas," he whispered against our soft melded lips.

"Bandit," I felt my throat thicken in emotion. "I've loved you since we were ten."

He chuckled while nuzzling my nose. "So, it's not just because of my exceptional good looks and colorful tattoos?"

I smiled and went to respond with a fantastic sassy retort but was interrupted by a knock. I winked at Bandit and turned my body to tuck myself between his legs. He wrapped an arm around my waist as I yelled for whoever it was to come in.

"Really?"

I smiled. Cosimo. The two of them were so similar sometimes.

"Oh, wow," Cosimo teased. "Way to keep it in your pants, Bandit."

"Actually," I drawled, "he does have pants on."

He raised a dark eyebrow. "And you?"

I smiled wickedly at him before motioning for a towel. He groaned but offered up the soft white material I needed to have wrapped around me. Bandit removed himself from the tub and discreetly adjusted himself. Cosimo had his back turned, so I offered him a salacious eyebrow wiggle that made him bark out a laugh.

My towel was in place before Cosimo turned around.

"Well, doesn't this look scandalous?" Booker commented softly from the doorway. He was dressed in comfortable clothes now. Specifically, an oversized black hoodie that I had purchased for him. It featured a graphic of his artwork.

"It doesn't just *look* scandalous. They were in the tub together," Cosimo laughed. It made me smile.

"Wonderful," Booker sighed with amusement. "Kids, do we need to have a safe sex talk?"

"God, no! The one with Vivi was awful enough!" I let out a soft laugh as Bandit smiled. Cosimo followed him out of the bedroom and left me with Booker. He jumped onto my bed and let out a massive groan. I smiled at him while tugging on an oversized shirt before dropping my towel. The shirt reached my knees, but I motioned for Booker to turn while I finished slipping on pants.

"I have seen you in less than what you are wearing now," he groaned, annoyed. He flattened, face down, on his stomach. I snickered and pulled on a pair of loose boy's boxers. My feet slid on the freshly washed flooring. I tumbled onto the bed and caught Booker in a body slam.

"Shit," he laughed. "You pack a little punch, muse."

I smiled at him before pressing my face into his hoodie. He sighed happily and wrapped the comforter around our melded forms. I felt him press his lips into my hair before speaking in soft tones.

"I thought he was going to pull the trigger, Vegas," he managed. "I thought I was going to lose you."

"Never," I claimed before grabbing a fistful of his shirt material.

He grunted and wrapped his legs around mine in a tight hold. We were wholly entwined with one another like two peas in a pod. The last thought I had before sleep consumed me was that for the first time all day, I felt perfectly safe.

That was how I should have known something was wrong.

Dawn brought fire and smoke.

Not metaphorically, either. I wasn't talking about the sun's daily journey across the sky. No, this fire was authentic...and burning. My hands trembled as I stood on our front porch. No one was up yet. No one had seen the text sent ten minutes ago.

A PRESENT FOR AN ARSONIST.

I hadn't heard that term in years. I hadn't seen a fire like this in years. I avoided it.

Now, I stood looking at the large fiery pattern that crossed over the dry autumn grass of our front lawn. I had my fingers on the numbers to dial 911 but just... didn't. Couldn't. The pattern of flames, viewable from my bedroom window, spelled out:

VEGAS

Good god. I could feel the heat flickering from here. The burnt orange and red heated tongues danced in tempting patterns. I wanted to join them. I wanted the fire to course through me until being cold and numb wasn't an option. Ever.

"Holy fuck," a voice yelled from the house. The whole house awoke. Texts were checked, and bodies moved toward the windows and doors. Everyone would see the present. Everyone would read the text.

"Vegas," Kodiak spoke cautiously from behind me. "How long have you been out here?"

"Ten minutes," I mumbled very softly. My throat was tight. Smoke danced around me. I could hear a fire engine driving in from town. My knees began to wobble.

"Inside. Now!" Blue demanded as Kodiak lifted me into his arms. My eyes never left the flames as he sat me in the living room. Everyone was exploding in action around me, but I couldn't express how I was feeling. Scared of my stalker but enthralled with the fire? How fucked up is that?

"Who the fuck else knows outside of the family?" I heard someone demand from the kitchen. My eyes flickered shut to block out the glee surging through me. I wanted back outside. That was bad.

Fire was bad.

I kept repeating the mantra, and each time it grew more difficult to believe. It was so fucking beautiful. So seductive. The flames were a siren to my soul. That wasn't normal, right?

"Beautiful," Blue demanded quietly. "You need to tell Rocket everyone you may have told."

I looked away from his baby blues to Rocket's steely gaze. He sat down on the couch and lifted my body onto his. I was turned away from the fire and felt myself frowning because of it. I began to panic.

"Turn her," Grover explained softly.

Rocket groaned and turned our bodies so I could gaze at the growing flames. My body tensed as the fire department pulled down into our driveway. They would put out the fire. They would destroy my fire.

"Who have you told sweetheart?" another voice asked softly.

"Stop them," I whispered urgently while looking out the window. "They are going to put out my fire. It was a present, and they are going to put it out."

I could feel panic bubbling through me as hot tears streamed down my face. Rocket began murmuring soft things in my ear, but it didn't help. I couldn't look away from the flames as they were extinguished. Was it that simple? That easy to destroy someone's flame?

A small sound of panic bubbled up from my chest as Grover's warm dark eyes appeared in front of my face. He took my jaw and turned it to face him fully. His tone was commanding and not one I heard often.

"Vegas. You have to snap out of it, angel. This isn't you anymore. You have to come back to us."

My eyes shut as the past unhooked itself from my subconscious and flew forward. The last sound I heard was a pained whimper emerge from my throat.

My fingers played a dangerous game. I leaned over the candle and swiped my hand through it. It wasn't enough to cause damage but enough that the flames licked my skin. I let out a small hum before turning away from the living room coffee table.

"Hey, Grover." I covered my startled reaction with a blank expression.

He didn't buy it. He continued to lean against the door frame with an unreadable expression dancing across his face. It wasn't a happy expression, and I feared he had seen me place my hand into the flames.

"Come here," he commanded. The house was quiet while everyone cleaned up for dinner. I could hear Lucida blasting music outside for her post cheerleading stretch session. Even that sound seemed faded though. Faded. Yes, that was a good word for how I felt since her death.

Better than empty. Not as bad as cold. Everything seemed so cold.

Except for fire. Fire would never be cold.

Just the word sent a thrill through me. It had since I was a little girl and all I had been doing was denying my affinity for it. I could set everything ablaze. I didn't know how but I could feel it instinctually. That man had tried to extinguish my fire. He had extinguished her fire. Now I could light a fire whenever I wanted. He was dead. He had no power. He had no fire.

One of my boys had put out his fire. They didn't have to tell me, I felt it in my bones.

Grover grasped my hand lightly. His auburn hair glinted in the sunset light that scattered across the living room floor. When had he gotten so tall? When had all of them gotten so tall? So big? How had I not noticed that? I supposed that was just one more thing I'd been ignoring.

"Angel," he whispered with darkening eyes. "You're scaring me."

"What?" I asked quietly snapping my eyes up in shock.

"This thing with fire," he murmured kissing my palm lightly. "It's scaring me. I didn't mind when it just seemed to be something you enjoyed, but it's different now. It's the only thing you pay attention to anymore."

I scared him? I didn't want to scare Grover. I loved Grover.

"It's not a big deal, honestly," I whispered. "I am working through it."

"It's been three months, angel," he mumbled quietly. "You need to talk to someone. The boys mentioned you have always played with fire. Is that true?"

Someone? Like who? Another unknown? Another stranger? I ignored his second comment.

"Shh," he grasped me in a tight hug as tears threatened to pour down my face.

"Can I just talk to you?" I whispered against his warm cheek. "Please? No strangers."

"Always, angel, always."

"We found a package left next to your front door. It contains lighters and gasoline." A deep voice commanded over the noise of the room.

My eyes fluttered open as early morning rays of light extended through the smoking, scorched front yard. My heart slowed as my breathing regulated. I could only manage to stare into Grover's large deep brown gaze. He was here. I would be okay. He would make sure I didn't burn anything down. I didn't want to hurt anyone.

So, why did it feel like I was denying my true nature?

"Thank you, officer, let us know if you find anything else," Booker's voice stood out to me. Officer? The police had arrived?

"Where is she?" A voice demanded.

"I need to see Vegas," the voice insisted. My vision blurred as I looked up at the rest of the room. I was still in Rocket's lap, and Grover shifted slightly to allow my path of sight to be cleared.

"B?" I mumbled in confusion. Well. That was unexpected.

His bright blonde hair stood in contrast to the faded dawn light. I could feel the entire room looking at us. The tension that rolled off my boys formed sickening waves. The police officers reacted accordingly by splitting up to cover all sides. I gripped Rocket's hand as a deep rumble slipped out from his throat.

"Vegas," B fell at my feet, literally, and lifted me from Rocket. His hug was too much. It was too warm. It was too intense for someone I barely talked to. Something was wrong, so wrong. Why did this hug feel familiar? Why wasn't I pushing him away?

Rocket hissed while pulling me back in a sharp movement. "Don't fucking touch her. We know what The Letters did last night." I was pushed behind Rocket as he leaned forward in a threatening manner.

The police held back almost everyone in the room. I could hear shouting and yelling. Something crashed as Grover was pulled back. A large hand came down onto B's shoulder. At least it was fair treatment. Everyone was being monitored. That was good, right?

"That wasn't me," he growled as flames flickered in his soft brown eyes and made them almost appear to be crimson. "If you think I would ever hurt her, you're fucking insane."

My head spun in confusion as my heart picked up a panicked rhythm. B studied my face before reaching out to touch my cheek. The touch was feather-soft. I felt a shiver journey through my spine.

"Okay, boys!" A strong, bold voice shouted. "Get the fuck out!"

I knew the newcomer who barged into our living room. She was my height. She had bright pink hair that was slicked back rather than curly. She was the girl who joined cheerleading just to date the captain. She was my best friend. She was my sister. Except this version of Lucida was nothing like the girl I had known since sixteen.

What in the actual fuck was going on? Was this a dream? That made sense.

She walked with determined steps and kept her gaze locked on mine. She wore a long tan trench and cropped pants with stilettos. The police began to shout for her to back up and she flipped open a black badge.

Alright, I was officially fucking confused.

"Pick up your damn phone," she snarled at a potbellied officer. "Your chief wants you out of here. Now."

My head rested gently on Rocket's shoulder as B kept his gaze locked on my face. I could feel the intensity radiating off Rocket. This was not the same man I had known since freshman year. At least Rocket was dependable. His arm wrapped around me and held me against his back with a strength that comforted me.

The police retracted their hands from my boys. Immediately a series of grunts and curses sounded through the room. Kodiak shoved a younger officer from his space as Blue stepped into another one's personal space while whispering. Whatever he said made the officer pale. Then they left.

They fucking left.

"Luci," I mumbled. She immediately stalked over, kicking B in the hip with her heel, and wrapping her arms around me. The scent of her soft poppy perfume surrounded me in a cloud of love and comfort.

"It's okay, Vegas," she promised. "We'll figure this out. I promise you."

"The badge?" I asked. Her eyes were heavy with concern, but those lips tilted in a small smile.

"I promise I will explain," she whispered. "Tonight. Dinner?"

I nodded. With that, Lucida was up and talking to the other boys spread throughout the room. My gaze fell back to B. He was still staring at me.

I wiggled away from Rocket as he grumbled under his breath. I sat on his knee and looked down at B who knelt at right below eye level. This dude was huge. My frown must have been apparent because he opened his mouth to offer commentary.

"Why are you here, B?"

Those brown eyes flickered with warmth. "Byron."

"What?" I asked with genuine confusion. Rocket stilled beneath me as the rest of the room was silent. Was a Letter telling me his real name? Holy guacamole. What in the fuckity-fuck was going on?

"My name," he sighed with exhaustion as if burdened with the weight of a secret kept too long. "My name is Byron."

"Oh," I inhaled with a swallow. "Why are you telling me this?"

"Because I like you."

Unease and silence filled the room. Byron smiled and lifted a hand to my cheek gently. "As to why I am here, I heard about the fire and immediately came over."

"How do we know he's not her fucking stalker?" Decimus mumbled with no heat. In fact, while the boys seemed cautious, they didn't seem to think Byron was an actual threat. Now, why did I feel like I was missing something here?

Byron rolled his eyes. "The same fucking reason I wouldn't put a hit out on Vegas."

I bit my lip nervously before falling back into Rocket's chest with a tired exhale. Byron offered me a soft smile and stood. He squeezed my hand gently, once more, before turning to leave. Lucida nodded at him in passing, and the boys parted to allow his exit. Yeah. Something was off here.

All eyes turned on me once he was gone. I didn't have anything to offer them though, so I closed my eyes. What a crazy fucking morning.

VEGAS

"**W**hat's with the bandage?" I asked curiously. Blue and I walked down campus drive with clasped hands. His ring finger was wrapped in white gauze. I wondered briefly if he had gotten rid of his tattoo. Why did that make me sad?

Blue smiled knowingly. "Don't worry, beautiful, I kept the tattoo."

I rolled my eyes. "I was just curious."

He chuckled at my response and led me toward the open student pavilion. It was an enclosed space with a glass roof that allowed for plentiful sunshine. I loved the area and was pleased to find Booker sitting at a small lunch table. Blue placed a hand on my lower back and led me toward him.

"Are you okay after this morning? We can go home," he whispered softly. I could tell he was on high alert as he looked around at the many students.

"I think you're more stressed than I am," I offered quietly.

He chuckled loudly. "No, shit. The woman I love is surrounded by potential stalkers and hitmen. You could say I'm stressed. It would be the understatement of the century."

I paused and turned to face him. Our chests bumped one another as my chin tilted back to see his mirth filled blue eyes. He smirked before grabbing hold of my shoulders in a stabilizing fashion.

"You love me?"

"What type of question is that?" He tilted his head in confusion. "Of course, I fucking love you, Vegas."

"Oh," I blushed a bright red. But did he mean he was *in* love with me? Or did he love me in that familiar way? What about Bandit? No. I *knew* Bandit was in love with me.

"What, beautiful?"

"Come on, you two!" Booker yelled. "Makeout later."

I grinned before tugging his hand toward the lunch table. My beautiful Booker sat looking polished in a three-piece autumn orange suit. I placed a soft kiss on his cheek before taking a seat next to him. Blue pulled out a pre-packed lunch and offered it to me.

"What's this?"

"Bandit packed your lunch. Eat something," he demanded. "I have to go make a call."

"Guess it's just you and me for lunch," Booker smiled brightly as Blue left the room. I instantly turned to face him as he mimicked my movement. He reached out to grasp my hand softly. The touch was loving and lighthearted.

Booker brought out a side of me that *was* lighthearted and playful. He made me feel as though life was sunnier than it seemed. His interests were beautiful and fascinating. He was complex yet expressed his emotions with an open-ness I envied.

"How's your day been?" Lame, Vegas. Lame.

"Well," he chuckled. "I can't beat this morning in interest, so fairly boring."

I nodded before popping a grape into my mouth. "I feel

like life has been crazy since I got sick. I keep assuming I'll wake up, and it will be a nice, boring Monday morning."

Booker sighed. "I wish, Vegas."

My hand found his soft blonde hair as I absently twirled a piece. He smiled broadly and leaned closer to me so that our noses gently brushed. A small butterfly sensation filled my gut as a blush flamed my cheeks.

"Well, maybe I don't because then we wouldn't be here," he whispered softly.

Our lips hovered inches apart as we both leaned over our lunchroom chairs. My inner school girl was squealing. Booker, my dashingly handsome friend, wanted to kiss me! Me! I could tell by how his velvet gray eyes tracked my lips like they were the most fascinating thing in the room.

"I didn't know you swung both ways, faggot."

Instantly the butterflies died. Literally fell dead into the pit of my stomach. They were replaced with venomous snakes that forced me to confront our assaulter. I sneered at K. My chair fell to the ground as I stepped in front of Booker in a fury. How dare he?

"Come on, Vegas," Booker encouraged softly but with slight amusement.

"K," I spoke dangerously soft. "I would be cautious. I've had your number for some time now. It's only a matter of time before I make my move."

K paled just enough to know I had made an impact. My eyes narrowed on his as a group of Letters joined him. I didn't pay them any mind. We were in the middle of the pavilion. What would they do? What could they do?

A chuckled. "Come on K, don't let this little human bitch..."

An explosion rocked through the entire building.

As the glass shattered, I pulled Booker toward me. Our

hands broke apart as a hard solid body slammed into mine with enough force that my head snapped back. The person cradled me against their chest and stopped my head from hitting against the marble flooring. Smoke and flames filled my senses. I tried to open my eyes but instead found a soft polo blocking my view. All I could see was lilac cotton.

"Vegas," a familiar voice snarled. "What the hell are you doing at school today?"

I pulled back and found myself staring into bright brown eyes. Levi? His hair was shorter than the day before and bruising still discolored his perfect skin. He had a wild and frankly manic look that plagued his gaze. I began to cough on smoke as he lifted me into his arms to stand.

"Booker," I coughed out. I couldn't see anything.

Levi didn't stop, though. Instead, he strolled through the closest emergency exit and into the fresh autumn air. I was curled against his chest as my breathing continued to be interrupted by coughing. He looked down with concern.

"I'm going to take you to the hospital," he mumbled quietly with guilt in his voice. What the fuck was he guilty about?

"Put her down, Levi," a chilling voice demanded. I looked up to find Rocket standing near Blue only inches away. Booker laid on the ground coughing but looked relatively unharmed.

Levi tightened his grip on me as he stared down Rocket's steely gaze. Another fit of coughs had me curling into a tight, uncomfortable ball.

"I can't breathe," I got out before Levi placed me on the ground gently. My coughing grew worse as I curled over myself on the chilly campus lawn. Booker's coughs echoed my own.

"What the fuck did you mean about her being in

152

school?" Rocket's bodiless voice asked quietly. Levi stilled behind me. A hidden microphone. I wasn't terribly surprised that the boys had a mic on me. Blue had mentioned upping security.

I would also like to point out, as the woman who notices everything, that I could not ignore the difference between this interaction and the one with Byron. I'm just putting it out there. I have no idea what the fuck it means but it is obvious that lately, I was definitely missing something. Cool. I love being left out of the loop.

"I heard about the fire this morning," he spoke in a low voice I had never heard before. "The Letters wouldn't shut up about it."

Suddenly, Rocket was in my line of sight. His multi-colored hair was messy and filled with dust. Those metallic eyes examined my face gently before he offered me a bottle of freshwater. I almost cried in relief.

"You need to leave," Blue spoke in a quiet deadly tone. "We've got them covered."

"I am not leaving her," he snarled tightly.

Rocket snarled softly before pulling my hair back into a twisted knot. I bet he did Booker's hair like this sometimes. He always needed help pulling back his hair while painting. I had done it more times than I could count and always would. I didn't want him to get frustrated with it and end up getting a haircut. I loved his hair.

"Levi," I spoke in a strangled tone, "I'll be fine. Go, make sure your other friends are okay."

He offered a series of curses before his footsteps sounded across the pavement. Instantly, my body relaxed and fell forward into Rocket's broad chest. He quickly picked me up and situated me on his lap in a protective hold. Well, it was more possessive than protective. I expected him to snarl if anyone got too close. I knew it had made him uncomfortable that Levi had been within a few feet of me even.

"He should be thrilled I haven't killed him yet," Booker muttered quietly. "He ripped us away from one another during the explosion. Rocket could have easily gotten both of us out."

"What was *that*?" I asked Rocket quietly. His soft button-down rubbed against my cheek gently as I nuzzled into him.

"A bomb."

"Why? Who?"

A silence fell from the others as Rocket tensed. I felt his arms tighten around me as he pressed a lingering kiss to the top of my head.

"I keep almost losing you," was all he managed.

I pulled back and frowned. What was I not understanding? Who would have had reason to bomb the school? They didn't think...

"That is exactly what I think," Blue responded with obvious concern. I swear he was a mind reader. It only made sense.

"You mean? All of those people may have, could have... died because of me?"

"What the fuck, Blue?" Grover demanded walking up. "You did not just fucking tell her that. What the hell is wrong with you?"

Blue frowned at his unusual outburst and looked at my face with interest. His eyes softened as he stalked forward and knelt on the ground to face me. Rocket soothed my hair gently with soft strokes as his chest rumbled. I waited for Blue to speak.

"This isn't your fault," he sighed with pain. "None of this is your fucking fault, but I won't hide my thoughts or opinions from you. Ever. I know you're strong enough to deal with this."

I was strong enough. Decimus offered me a look from Booker's side that steeled my resolve. I nodded and pressed a gentle kiss to Rocket's cheek before standing up. He didn't let go though. Rocket was a quieter person compared to the others, but he never shied away from physical contact with me. Even now, his hands held my waist tightly.

"Baby," Kodiak demanded softly from Rocket's side. I turned to see my big grizzly bear looking down at me with evident concern and frustration. I reached a hand out to brush his cheek with soft affection. He leaned down and pressed a sweet sugar-filled kiss to my lips.

I tried to deepen it, but Rocket's arms and slight growl prevented me. I turned to him with a raised brow. Shit, I was kissing another man while in his arms. That's awkward. Right? This should be weird. Why didn't it feel weird?

"Rocket, I..."

Kodiak broke into a deep chuckle and rolled his sparkling eyes. "Stop giving her a hard time, you possessive freak."

"I resent those two words together," Blue called out from another conversation. My eyes were focused on Rocket though. He didn't seem upset. Instead, he appeared needy. Hungry. His grey eyes sparkled in a predatory fashion that caused my heart to swell with excitement.

"It's true," Rocket explained while nuzzling my neck. "I am jealous."

His large hands turned me into his chest. I placed my hands on his shoulders in a soothing motion that caused him to shiver. His head tilted down to mine in a slow, meticulous move.

"Jealous?"

"That was his second kiss, and I haven't even had one," he explained gently.

I flushed. "Oh."

He smiled with intent and leaned forward so that our lips touched lightly. Now, I would like to state that this could have been a light, playful kiss. It could have been a swift brush of our mouths.

But this was *Rocket and me*, so it was anything but that.

"Holy shit!" A voice called out from our group.

My nails dug into Rocket's shoulder as the ground around us exploded in tectonic movements. Our lips met in a rough kiss that was aggressive and nearly animalistic. I could feel a whimper working its way from my throat as those large hands slipped beneath my thighs. I locked my legs around his hips the moment my back hit the brick wall behind us. Rocket let out a deep growl against my lips that sent every part of my body spiraling toward the unknown.

The world was breaking apart from underneath me because of a kiss. This wasn't a bomb going off. It was the world splitting. Rocket's firm lips took everything I offered and then demanded more. Our hips ground together as some innate, primal desire encouraged me to strip here and now, despite the audience.

The audience.

"Oh, fuck," I pushed back slightly. I breathed in his mint scent and found myself staring into a very expressive version of Rocket. His face held a myriad of emotions. I had never been looked at with so much possession and ownership. I felt like a marked woman. A claimed woman.

What the fuck had just happened?

"We need to leave," Grover stated quietly. It was then that I realized the other men had formed a wall around us. My sweet boys.

Rocket let out a territorial growl against my neck before placing me on the ground. His arm locked around my waist as we turned to walk back down campus drive. My eyes trailed behind me in wonderment. I had completely forgotten about the bomb.

Oh, right. The bomb that may or may not have been my fault. That rabbit hole theory was sounding much better.

14

LUCIDA

"Sweetheart," I whispered. "After this job, things will change. I promise."

"Alright, Luci," the soft, familiar voice responded. "I will call you after work."

"I love you."

"Love you more."

My heart ached when it was away from Miranda. Even after a moment of talking to her, my heart beat an irregular rhythm. It could have also been the coffee.

The arson case this morning had been upsetting, to say the least. More so, the terrified look on Vegas's face. My best friend wasn't scared easily. She lived with a house of eight testosterone-filled fools. It wasn't for the faint of heart. Yet, she handled it with ease. She always had. It helped that every single one of them was in love with her.

When I had first arrived in Ohio, I hated it. Small. Conservative. Boring. I hadn't had a choice though. There was nowhere else to go. When I had met Vegas, my opinion drastically changed. She had accepted me without question.

She had never questioned my sexual preferences. She had never examined my past.

Vegas had just stuck her hand out and invited me to spray paint the boy's headboards a bright neon green. Vivian had nearly had our hide for that.

Now, she was in trouble. Someone was gunning for her, and it was putting her life in danger as well as distracting us from finishing our job. Everything about the situation had escalated tenfold since Monday. Somehow I knew it would only become worse before it became better.

My phone rang with an eerie tone.

"Nice to fucking hear back from you," I snarled into the phone.

"Lucida," the voice chided.

"No," I snapped. "You overstepped today. You know it."

A deep sigh echoed through the connection. "I know. I just couldn't. Either I showed up or my brother did."

I paused at that last. That would have been a fucking terrible option. I could deal with this fool but the few times I had met with his brother had been, let's just say...interesting. That was a nice description of how it went.

"Fix it. We need to finish this job," I mumbled while leaning against my cluttered kitchen island. Vegas would have a fucking conniption if she saw the state of my apartment.

"I'll text you when we are good to go."

"Okay. Bye." I hung up the phone in frustration.

A knock sounded on my front door. It was around noon, but the visit was unusual considering my apartment was outside of town. I check my gun, making sure the safety was off, before opening the door.

What the hell?

15

BOOKER

I played gently with the soft silky strands that fell loose from Vegas's braid. She sat with pursed lips and a cute little crease in the middle of her forehead. I could tell she was deep in thought. Rightly so, but I just didn't have the focus that she had. My thoughts were far more fluid and less focused.

"That tickles," she smiled as I leaned over and pinned her against the hospital bed.

She claimed to feel perfectly fine, but Neanderthals One through Seven, in the waiting room, had insisted she be checked out. As we waited on the doctor, I continued my attempt to leave her smiling permanently.

"What tickles?" I asked with mock confusion. My teeth gently tugged on her ear this time as a strangled gasp giggle slipped from her mouth.

"Booker," she whined with amusement. "Stop it."

"Stop what?" I asked again. This time my nibble landed at her collar bone. The hospital gown she wore was hideous, but her curves were far more noticeable in the thin material.

I hoped the doctor was a woman. For the sake of the doctor, of course.

"Booker," she grasped my jaw and tilted it up. She frowned but couldn't hide her amusement. Good. I hated seeing her in this damn hospital bed.

In my opinion, the only time someone should be in a hospital bed is to give birth. Any other time it's terrible news. I smiled at Vegas and ignored my thoughts of birth, and more specifically, her giving birth. How the hell was that going to work? We had never talked about that aspect of our family in detail.

"What are you thinking about?" she asked quietly. Her eyes were filled with questions as she attempted to unravel my soul.

"Kids, actually," I mumbled. Why bother lying? She would know. We had enough lies between us right now.

"Oh?" she asked with a goofy smile.

I fucking blushed and folded my elbows so that we were a nose apart. "Yes. My theory on hospitals is that, unless you're giving birth, you shouldn't be here. Any other reason is usually due to some terrible event."

Vegas smiled with gleaming teeth and let out a laugh. "I actually agree with that."

"Do you want to have kids one day?" I asked. My curiosity had gotten the better of me. I couldn't help it around her.

"Of course," she smiled. "Our family has made me so happy already, I can only imagine what throwing a few kids in the mix would do."

How did she not hear herself? She had to know. I knew she didn't though, not entirely. Yet she spoke about our family's future with such certainty. Those indigo eyes sparkled with interest as she began to describe, in impressive detail, her plan for the holidays.

"You see," she explained. "I just keep imagining Christmas morning, with presents and a huge breakfast laid out, where all the kids are opening presents. Then all of us would be able to..."

I wanted her to keep going but she paused. Her lip jutted out unintentionally as those large eyes glossed over for just a moment. It was a slip in her reactions, but I knew where her mind had gone. I also knew that if I ever told her she was pouting, she'd probably gut me. I had tried telling her once that I liked her giggle and she had ended up tackling me to the floor. She had forced me to admit that I h*ad never and would never* hear her giggle.

She did, often. It didn't take away from how tough she was.

"I suppose though," she sighed, "if all of you have families, you will be with them. Not me."

I tilted my head and moved closer, just slightly. "What if that's not the case?"

She frowned. "Booker, what do you mean?"

"What if," I paused with confusion on how to move forward. "I mean, we already have a unique relationship, the nine of us. So, would it be that far fetched to imagine..."

"Imagine what?"

"*Us.* All of us."

Those dark brows shot up as her pretty eyes turned more purple than blue. I didn't see disgust or fear though. I saw confusion. I could work with confusion. "I am sure the others..."

"Vegas?" A deep baritone called her name as a jolt of familiarity coursed through me. I looked up at the disruptive guest and found my eyes widening in surprise.

Oh, shit.

VEGAS

My eyes flew from Booker's surprised expression to the man I assumed to be my doctor. Except that seemed unlikely because doctors weren't usually this young...*right?* The man that strode into the room could have only been twenty-six at most.

He wore his thick black shoulder-length hair in a braid that looked professional yet unbearably sexy on him. His skin was a beautiful olive tone that sparkled beneath the fluorescent lighting and showcased his masculine features. He was a beautiful man, and that was before his gaze found mine from behind dark-rimmed glasses.

Holy crap.

He had orange eyes. I mean they must have been brown, realistically, or maybe hazel, but they really looked orange. Like a burnt pumpkin orange surrounded by thick dark lashes. As I continued my perusal, his small smile turned into a large overwhelming smile. Booker let out a low rumble as he stepped closer to the two of us. The closer he moved, the more my body tensed. Not out of fear but recognition. I felt like I knew this man and that was fucking impossible but I could never forget that face.

"Vegas," he smiled in greeting. "I'm Edwin, one of the residents here. I just wanted to check one or two things before I give Dr. Morris the green light. There are a lot of kids here today because of the bombing, so we've had to split up the work."

"Sounds good to me," I smiled feeling comfortable around him. Booker made another pained noise that caused Edwin to smile further. There was a darkness to this man

163

like the shadows clung to him, but it didn't bother me. No, not at all. I think he felt something as well because behind the smile there was confusion and pain in his gaze that trailed over my face.

I tried to ignore the soft scent of smoke that surrounded me in his proximity. He worked quietly but with a precision that was clearly practiced. The nurse had done most of the heavy work, so I assumed it wouldn't take very long. I was eager to get home and ask Booker about the scowl on his face.

"How are the guys doing?"

Booker looked up with a strained smile. "Pissed that the nurse only let one of us back."

"Hospital regulation," Edwin spoke in a sing-songy voice. He was an odd one. I briefly wondered if I had said that out loud because his lip twitched in amusement.

"I assumed that as well, originally," Booker snarled softly before going back to his phone. This was so not like Booker. Why did he dislike Edwin so much?

"Is that a tattoo?" I asked with genuine curiosity. My distraction worked.

Edwin broke into a broad smile before answering. When he finished with my vitals, he rolled up his sleeve to reveal a forearm tattoo of impressive size.

"A red mask?" I felt as though my words didn't do the artwork justice. It was a beautiful piece that could only be rivaled by Bandit's expansive fantasy piece.

"Something like that," he grinned salaciously. "It's from one of my favorite works."

The more he talked, the more I caught hints of an accent. It almost sounded Eastern European and reminded me faintly of another voice I'd heard recently. I just couldn't connect who I was thinking about.

"Oh! The Masque of the Red Death?" I asked with excitement. I loved Edgar Allan Poe. Edwin tilted his head back and let out a deep chuckle in response to Booker's curse. I looked at my friend with confusion, but he avoided eye contact and continued to type furiously. I turned back to Edwin and found his orange gaze far closer than before. His muscular forearms landed on either side of me as my heart began to beat quicker.

"What do you know about Edgar Allan Poe?" he asked with genuine interest. My answer seemed essential to him. Once again, behind that smile there were hints of deep raw pain that I could only assume were connected to me in some way. Had I hurt him? Had I met him before and forgotten? No. That wouldn't have been possible.

I started to reply but Booker beat me to it, "Edwin. You have a call."

A low rumble broke from my doctor's chest as he turned to stare down at Booker. It was very obvious to me that they knew one another. How?

"How long have you known one another?" I asked.

Edwin smiled, "Yes, Booker. How long have we know one another?"

Booker paled and looked back down. My frown must have been apparent because Edwin cooed gently. "Don't you worry, little raven. I will tell you the truth. Always."

Suddenly, Edwin's name was called over the speaker system. A flash of something crossed his face before he returned to his devil-may-care grin. He brushed my cheek. "Until then, dear Vegas, stay safe."

My doctor was gone. Booker was silent, and I was terribly confused. A nurse came in to usher Booker out while I changed. I felt eager to leave the hospital.

My footsteps echoed down the long hallway that led to

the waiting room. I hadn't stepped one foot into the lobby before my body was engulfed in the best double hug I had ever experienced. Cosimo and Bandit held me close and I realized how worried they had been. I understood because if I had gotten a call about one of them being in the hospital, I would have been terrified.

"I am so glad you're okay," Cosimo expressed with soft kisses to my neck. Bandit pressed a sweet electrifying kiss to my lips before pulling away. The two of them together brought imagery to my mind I had never considered before.

As we walked to the car, my thoughts wandered over my experience in the hospital. What had Booker been talking about? All of us together? Did he really mean that? Was it even possible? I couldn't be that selfish, could I? Who was Edwin? Why did Booker hate him so much? What had he meant about telling me the truth? Was there a lie affecting my life?

I distracted myself with Rocket's baritone voice.

"I was able to log into their system," he explained. "It seems that the product we tested in the lab was found in several of the students admitted for injuries. It's spreading through the school."

"What's spreading?"

Both of them looked at me and paled. Instead of explaining though they went quiet.

Okay, boys.

I had run out of patience with this game.

"Booker," I demanded quietly. "Want to tell me who Edwin is?"

We had been getting into the car, and my words had brought everyone and I do mean everyone, to a halt. Blue's eyes met mine with a look that seemed almost fearful.

"Well?" I asked the group quietly. Everyone looked at

Blue. His face instantly blanked as he crossed his arms to lean comfortably against the car.

"Someone we met this summer," he explained.

I let out a low growl. "Yeah? And let me guess. Everyone met him except me?"

"He's not a good guy," Kodiak offered in a softer voice than usual.

"Okay." I inhaled once before laying out my cards. "I know something is going on. Something has changed since May, and I need to know what and why. I gave you more than enough time, but it's nearly November now. We are family and family doesn't lie to one another. So I am about done waiting for answers."

Bandit wrapped an arm around my waist as his eyes narrowed on Blue. Everyone else seemed to defer toward him as well, which meant only one thing. Blue had been the one who had decided not to tell me.

"Blue?" I could hear the hurt in my voice.

"Later," he exhaled with a tired sigh. "You're having dinner with Lucida tonight, right? We can just make it a family dinner instead."

"Okay," I nodded in confirmation. The tension seemed to ease as we crawled into the car and made our way home.

I sent a quick text to Lucida about dinner before looking out my side window. Rocket strummed his fingers against my leg in a soothing motion. The small suburban college town outside of Boston had changed colors within the past month. I took the time to appreciate the many shades of brown, red, and yellow that littered the beautiful collegiate campus. In that singular moment, I felt my doubts slip away, and a strange butterfly feeling of contentment filled my chest. I appreciated it while I could.

It only lasted moments, though.

Lucida hadn't texted me back about dinner, and the car had grown quiet with tension. I knew the boys, notably Blue, was frustrated about having to tell me. Either that or they planned on lying to me. Either way, it was an uncomfortable situation. As we parked, the car cleared out in record time as everyone began to split off to their respective rooms. I stood in the foyer with confusion and hurt palpitating through my chest. How dangerous could the secret be that they couldn't stand to be around me? Tears streamed down my face as I turned toward the door. Our family never had secrets. Why was this different?

I stepped into the cold autumn air and pulled the front door shut quietly. I still wore my clothing from class this morning. A pair of dark jeans with a soft lilac sweater and my black, fall shearling jacket. I had even added a pair of small black heeled boots. It was a great outfit that had me feeling fantastic this morning. Now? Now, I didn't give a fuck. I leaned my head back against the closed door and let some silent frustrated tears continue to fall.

I didn't want them to see me crying about this. Normally, I wouldn't have cared but them keeping something from me made me feel distant. Removed from them. Then again, that may have been because of the bomb and meeting Edwin. Now, some type of secret hung over our group. My head dipped in confusion as I reached my small sedan and turned on the nearly silent ignition.

I needed out of the house, if even for a few moments. My thoughts turned to possible stress relief solutions as I drove into town. My car found itself in front of the only place I knew would make me feel better. It would also showcase to the Ravens how upset I truly was. In this case, I let the good outweigh the bad.

"How can I help you, Miss?"

"I need a change," I demanded softly. The woman's eyes lit up as she immediately led me back toward a vanity stand. Her hair, a soft metallic blue, hung right above her shoulders. It was adorable but not something I felt comfortable with.

"What were we thinking?"

"Bangs," I nodded with confidence, "Straight bangs."

She smiled, "I think that will look absolutely adorable on you."

Her hands were practiced as she began to shampoo my hair with soft rosemary-scented soap. My eyes closed as peaceful music trickled through my ears. I had been to this spa many times before but never for a haircut. However, the minute her scissors touched my hair, a sense of calm overtook me. This was precisely what I had needed.

ROCKET

My entire body shook with anticipation that had nothing to do with our current argument. No, this electric feeling that made my body vibrate had everything to do with Vegas. Instead, I was stuck being subjected to this discussion. Booker and Bandit were heavily involved in a debate with Decimus as Blue stalked around the room restlessly. Grover and Kodiak both spoke in low tones that seemed to exist below the typical hearing spectrum. Cosimo stood next to me and fidgeted with his lip piercing. Out of everyone, he seemed to be the most anxious about Vegas's possible reaction to our little secret. The secret that had caused all of this mounting tension and anxiety.

"Fuck it. We're just going to fucking tell her," Blue sighed, "We don't have an option anymore. Any arguments?"

"Thank fucking god," Bandit sighed. "I hate keeping shit from her."

"Which reminds me," Booker commented. "There is something else that we have been keeping from her that we need to admit to."

"I want her to realize it herself," Blue complained quietly.

"She won't. She will think it's way too selfish to even consider," Cosimo offered.

"Won't she freak out? I mean it's not exactly the norm, what we are suggesting," Grover sighed before throwing himself down on the living room sofa.

"No," Booker explained. "She's already in the correct mindset. She just hasn't realized it."

"What do you mean?" Kodiak asked with interest. I could tell he wanted to hunt down Vegas. She had disappeared somewhere, presumably upstairs, after our tense conversation in the car. I had seen the pained expression on his face and could only imagine that he felt the same level of guilt I did. I hated lying to her.

Booker sighed before launching into an explanation of what had occurred in the hospital. My thoughts skimmed briefly over the details about Edwin but focused far more on the comments regarding family and children. Specifically, Vegas having children. My children. Our children. It didn't really matter. The idea was appealing.

"Get that look off your face, Rocket," Booker warned. "You look like a caveman."

My head swiveled back with raised brows. "Okay but biologically speaking..."

Kodiak chuckled. "You're just looking for a reason to tie her to us permanently."

"Is that a bad thing? Biologically speaking, it makes sense that we would want..."

Blue grinned. "Don't bring your science bullshit into this Rocket. You're just a possessive fuck. Not that I care, honestly, if there were a way for her to marry all of us, I would be the first to suggest it."

"Biologically," I explained again as my patience grew thin, "my possessiveness makes sense. We take care of what is ours. Protect what is ours. Vegas is ours, so why wouldn't I want to tie her to us in every way possible?"

Cosimo snorted and walked toward the living room window, "well jeez Rocket when you say it like that."

"It's a brilliant idea, actually. She'll never leave if we have a big family. There will be too many people who love her," Grover said with a distant look in his eyes.

I could see the concept of our vast family sinking in. No one in the group seemed to have given a lot of thought to the happily-ever-after of our group.

I had. Often.

"Oh, man. Do you think we would be good dads?" Bandit perked up with a thoughtful look. I grinned at his sudden enthusiasm.

Decimus chuckled. "Yeah? Maybe? Shit, I don't know. What makes a good dad?"

A howl of cynical laughter went through the room as Grover rasped out, "oh shit, none of us knows shit about parenting."

Booker rolled his eyes and looked at me. "Well, a good element of it may be telling the potential mom we even want to have kids with her."

Cosimo sighed. "She should really know how we feel before we throw all this other shit on her."

Blue nodded. "Go find her."

I sat back and took a long look around the room. Could I imagine being a co-parent with these guys? Yes. I couldn't do it alone. I knew that. Could I imagine Vegas as a mother? Absolutely. She would be a fantastic mother. She was strong-willed yet loving. I could imagine her fantasy just as Booker had described. Christmas morning? Presents? All of us together? Yeah, I would be down for that.

Another very primal part of me wanted to brand her perky little ass. I wanted my stamp on it, declaring that she was mine. If I couldn't do that shit with a ring than one day, I would do it with a family. I would give her the family she wanted and anything else. I had been hooked since first meeting her, but after that kiss, something had changed. I could feel her kiss still on my lips. I could feel her energy pulsating through me and encouraging me to find her.

She was ours, and I would give anything to make sure she stayed.

"Guys," Cosimo's voice sounded panicked. "She's not home."

"What?" Kodiak growled.

"Her car is gone. Fuck," Grover yelled from the foyer.

Where had she gone?

VEGAS

"I love it," I smiled happily. My silver hair hung down to my waist in a straight fresh line, and my bangs curled across my forehead in soft wispy strands. It looked perfect. I felt all my anger and frustration subside.

After I left the salon, I found myself heading toward a local coffee shop called Beans. While my anger had subsided, I still hadn't a clue on how to handle the boys or Lucida. I felt hurt and confused that they would keep something from me. I also rationalized that they had probably kept it from me for a good reason. I hoped that was the case. If it hadn't been for Booker's odd reaction to Edwin, I could have even assumed that it was something internal. Like maybe how I had kissed five of my eight boys in the past twenty-four hours? No. Edwin had ruined that theory.

Damn. Ignorance was bliss.

"Vegas?" A smooth voice asked.

I turned to come face to chest with Nathan leaving Beans. I immediately broke out into a huge smile that made his eyes light up. His honey-colored eyes looked more intense today, more alive than they usually did. He seemed happy.

"Hey, you," I chirped while offering him a tight hug. Those massive arms wrapped around me in a warm hold that lifted my feet off the pavement.

"Did you change your hair?" he asked curiously. My feet touched back down, but his arms didn't leave my waist.

"I got bangs," I smiled authentically.

"They look great. I mean, you always look beautiful, Vegas but wow!" He grinned with a slight blush tinging his cheeks.

Nathan was sweet. He was open, honest, and always complimentary. I had always wondered why I couldn't feel for him what I felt for my boys. Instead, Nathan left me with a sense of familiar brotherhood. Essentially, my brain was all fucked up, and I desired my foster brothers but couldn't view my handsome friend as anything more than a brother.

When they were putting together the parts in my head, they may have messed something up.

"How are you after last night?" he asked quietly. "Everything okay at home? I don't see any of the guys around."

I sighed. "I went out without telling them. I just needed some time to think."

He nodded and twisted his lips in thought. "Want to come back to my apartment and hide out for a bit? I have that new Spyro game."

"Absolutely," I nodded.

Nathan lived in an apartment above his family's bar but rented a studio place in downtown as well. When I asked him about the additional purchase, he had explained the need for space. Space away from what I wasn't sure. I followed him toward the three-story brick complex and found myself entranced with the beautiful landscaping.

"This is a great place," I smiled at him. "Your landlord knows his shit."

He grinned. "I'll be sure to let myself know."

"You own this building?"

Nathan's eyes glinted in the sun as he opened the main door. "I have a knack for investments. It's sort of becoming my thing."

"Wow," I whispered. "That's impressive, Nathan."

He blushed again and opened a sizeable blue door to the right side of the massive, modern foyer. It was a stunning structure. The walls were a pale silver and the floors a sleek blue, patterned tile. A vase of bright blue roses sat front and center next to the staircase. I turned my attention from the foyer to the blue door.

"Damn, Nathan," I whispered, stepping into the studio apartment.

It deserved a "damn." I barely heard the door lock behind me as I started to explore the space. I felt a flutter of excitement pool in my stomach at the thought of spending time here. The walls were tall and painted in a deep gold that complimented the heavy orange curtains that kept the room cozy. While no sunlight broke through the seemingly massive windows, there was a warmth and energy to the room. I ran my hands along the stone fireplace, sadly unlit, and looked to the impressively large purple silk bed that sat to the far corner. The entire room reminded me of a low burning flame. It sparked something in me.

"Okay, so are you a mind reader? Or maybe my secret twin I didn't know about?" I grinned with enjoyment at his frown about being siblings. It didn't take away from the intense gaze he aimed at me from the end of his large bed.

"Why?" he grinned knowingly.

"If I had money, this would be my room," I stated authentically. "Actually, screw the money. It's mine. I am officially claiming it, and you're moving out."

Nathan stepped forward with amusement sparkling in his eyes. "How about this? You have it for free, and I don't move out?"

I frowned in confusion but let out a small laugh. "Trust me. You don't want to live with me. I'm a mess and live with eight even messier men."

Nathan licked his lips and looked down at me with a gentle expression. "I can handle your mess. I wouldn't mind a bit."

"You want to live with me?"

"I want a lot of things Vegas," he stated in a tone of voice I had never heard before. "Most of them have to do with you."

I felt my breathing halt as I chose my words carefully. "I think you may have eight other people who might disagree with me moving out."

Fire lit in those amber eyes as he clutched my shoulders in a tight grasp. "Screw them, Vegas. I know they sometimes scare you into agreeing with them."

Alright. This wins. This is the fucking weirdest conversation I've had since Monday.

I felt my eyes widen at his malice. "Nathan, those are my family members you're talking about."

He let out a sharp growl before turning around. His aggressive energy had me realizing just how alone I was with him and how large he was compared to me.

"I could be your family, Vegas," he pleaded suddenly. "We don't need them. I promise I've worked hard to be good enough for you on my own. I could be everything for you."

My heart rate picked up as I tried to examine and think

through this situation. "What are you talking about, Nathan?"

"These past three years," he mumbled in a low tone, "I've worked so hard to be enough, to be more than them. I kept the bar because you visited there, but I've done so much more than that. I bought this entire house for us. I did it all for you. For us."

Oh, sweet baby Jesus. I have to be dreaming 'cause today has been a fucking nightmare.

"Holy shit, Nathan," I murmured. "Why did you do that?"

The sneer that took over his lips was enough to scare me. "I love you, Vegas. I always have. I knew it wouldn't be easy to save you from them. I knew they hadn't touched you, so I bided my time. But on Monday, I saw him kiss you, Vegas! He kissed *my* lips. I knew the time had come. Then you, my beautiful little rose, just appeared out of thin air. Don't you see? You knew where home was and came of your own accord. I didn't even need to break in."

"You're my stalker?" I whispered through a thick, strangled voice.

"I'm your future husband, not your fucking stalker," he sneered again. His body moved forward, and within seconds, I was plastered to his chest. Except this hug was forced. This wasn't the Nathan I loved. This man was scary.

"Nathan," I whispered as tears claimed my eyes. "Don't do this. I need to go home, and you need to think through what you're saying."

"You're not leaving, little rose," he whispered with emotion. "Ever. I have spent years thinking this through, and I could never lie to you about how I feel. You're my obsession, Vegas. You're my entire world."

"Let me go," I mumbled against his chest. I considered

trying to scratch out his eyes or punch him but had a feeling that he would physically overpower me. I didn't want to put myself in a worse position. No. I needed to think this through.

"I will put you down, but until you realize the reality of our new life, I can't let you out. I don't want them finding you," he mumbled again.

I pulled away and moved back, my knees breaking over the edge of the large bed. A shiver ran through me at the implications, but he must not have noticed it. Instead, Nathan went to light a fire in the massive stone fireplace. My heart began beating in anxiety and excitement.

"Stop," I whispered. I didn't want to feel excitement from the fire.

"You love fire," he frowned. "I saw it this morning."

A soft small pained sound worked its way up my throat as my knees broke. He frowned more but continued to work the fire until it began a low burn. My pulse began to beat at the same rhythm that the flames licked the surrounding stone.

With as much effort as I could manage, I walked toward the door and pulled uselessly. I knew it was locked. I just... I had to show him that I wanted to leave. It hurt so much. *Nathan*. I had lost Nathan the minute he had started talking. Losing someone you love always broke your heart.

"Vegas," Nathan demanded my attention. I turned as his hands came around the door to trap me. "You don't want to go back to them. They scare you. They lie to you."

"They have never hurt me," I snarled quietly. Anger slowly replaced the hurt.

"And the lies?"

I swallowed hard but kept my face blank. I immediately began searching the room and his person for the key. I didn't know if he knew what I was doing or not. It was times like this that I was thrilled by how much I noticed.

"I found out some interesting information about your Ravens," he explained. His significant form laid out across the massive bed as he motioned for me to sit on the edge of it. I bit my lip and approached. He had to have the key. I needed the key.

"What's that?" I leaned toward Nathan with interest. I kept my reactions to a minimum so that he didn't grow suspicious.

"They joined a new group in May," he lamented with a stretch that raised his shirt. "And they didn't even tell you, little rose. They excluded you."

That hurt. That hurt a whole fucking lot. Reminder – kick all of them in the balls.

"What group?" I asked with open eagerness. I made sure to give an exhausted sigh before falling back onto the bed next to him. His eyes dilated just enough to know I had affected him.

"I don't know the name but their info routes back to an office overseas," he explained with pride.

I nodded and closed my eyes. "So, they lied to me, and were going to leave me?"

"Yes," he clung to my bullshit like a big fat fly. "That is exactly what they would have done to you, little rose. My beautiful little rose."

His large hand brushed my cheekbone and caused my skin to break out in shivers. Not the toe-curling shivers either. These shivers were filled with disgust.

"Thank you," I whispered before pressing a kiss to his cheek. A sigh of contentment came from those lips that had given me so many friendly smiles.

"Why did they kiss me if they were going to leave me?" That should get a reaction.

"They? I thought it was only Blue," he snarled. Nathan was instantly on his elbow and looming over me. I tried to keep my pulse regulated as my breathing increased in tempo. I was in control here. I was in control. I repeated it again and again.

Something was off here. How had he not known about Kodiak? Hadn't he sent the damn photo? *No.* There was something odd here.

"No, five of them have kissed me in the past day," I explained softly.

A look of fury crossed Nathan's face before a mask of calm trickled back in. I wouldn't be fooled though. His pulse was beating quickly and those warm eyes were like hard stones.

"I don't know why," I whispered. "They never said they liked me."

Love is different than like? Right?

My hand gently grasped his jaw as my other trailed his hip. He groaned at my touch and fell back onto the bed. I rolled with him so that I was straddling his massive form. I tried to not let my unbelievable disgust with this situation show on my face.

For the record, I was going to fucking kill my boys. After I told them how much they mean to me.

"Fuck, little rose," he whispered, looking over my slender form. "You're so small. I don't want to hurt you."

Yep. There was the vomit.

"We can work up to it. No need to rush, right?" I batted my eyelashes like a good girl. I could taste the bile in the back of my throat and began to feel dizzy.

"If I was a smart man," he mumbled, "I would lock you to me in every way possible."

Oh, fuck, no.

"Wouldn't it be better if we had a real relationship?" I hoped. His possessive nature made me feel sick in comparison to my boys. That was saying something since Blue was certifiable. I loved that about him though.

"You're right," he whispered.

I moved forward, grasped the key in his pocket, and kissed Nathan. Luckily, he barely noticed my missing right hand as I tucked the key into the back of my jeans. See Kodi? Bandit's lessons on how to pickpocket had worked in my favor. I made sure to deepen the mildly warm kiss before pulling back.

"That was so much better than I imagined," he whispered with hooded eyes.

I offered a bright smile before tucking myself into his side. Those large palms smoothed my hair back in attempted comfort. Instead, I felt sick. So sick.

"I can use the washroom here, right?" I mumbled softly.

"Of course," he nodded.

The bathroom was beautiful. A soft blue and orange tiled pattern that made my heart patter in excitement. I loved these colors and the fucker knew that. Except nothing could replace how I felt around fire. Well, maybe sex, but that wasn't the point.

I turned on the sink and opened the medicine cabinet. I grinned when I found a package of Benadryl. That should do the fucking trick. I crushed it up quickly and dissolved it into a glass of water he had offered me. Once the water was clear, I placed a straw in the water and pretended to take a drink.

"All good?" he asked happily. I nodded, taking a pretend sip and sat on the edge of the bed. Nathan grasped my waist from behind, and I took the opportunity. My body turned as an elbow knocked his throat just enough. He coughed as I uttered apologizes and patted his back. I offered him the water as he began to suck it down in earnest. Fuck! For a smart guy, he really was terrible at kidnapping people.

This cemented my theory that Nathan wasn't my stalker. Well. Not the one leaving dead birds, creepy photos, and burning lawn messages. He was 100% still a stalker. An obsessive stalker who had created his version of Willy Wonka's fantasyland for me. Who knew I had such a thing for decor? Apparently, he had.

"Thanks, love," he mumbled before falling back onto the bed. "Sexy, right?"

"I think you're pretty sexy," I mumbled unconvincingly under my breath while looking away. I could practically feel this guy's peacock feathers spreading. Asshole.

"Wait," I mumbled quietly. "If you left me the birds and present? Was the bomb you as well?"

Nathan's eyes darkened. "No. I would never put you in danger."

"Oh," I nodded. "Good. Very good." Did I believe him? Maybe? He was creepily honest. I briefly remembered Levi's comment about me being in school.

"Want to take a nap? I can show you the rest of the house later," he explained.

Before I could respond, he pulled me into the bed and spread the large silky blanket over us. I breathed in his scent. The one that had always made me smile but would now forever be associated with captivity. Fuck this. This was fucked up.

MY EYES STAYED TRAINED on the fire. I focused only on the fire. Nathan was just another one who wanted to extinguish my flame. I was not a prisoner. I would get out of here.

It was only an hour later that I was confident Nathan was sleeping. My movements were slow and lazy as I got up. I acted as though I was heading toward the bathroom. After a few moments, assured he wouldn't wake, I moved toward the door. My hands slipped into the back of my pants as I wiggled the key from my spine into my hand.

The moment of truth was oddly anti-climactic. A snore tumbled from his lips as I snorted quietly and unlocked the door. *Damn.* I was laughing at my stalker. I slipped out the door as soon as the lock clicked open. With care, I closed the heavy blue door gently. A relieved breath came from my chest.

Shit.

I just slipped away from my kidnapper. I was suddenly filled with a sense of pride. For the second time in my life, I had avoided captivity. I had avoided being a prisoner.

A hand clasped over my mouth. I screamed.

"Princess," Decimus gently bit my ear. "I love you but shut your sexy mouth."

Relief exploded from my chest as I turned into his grasp and hooked my legs over his hips. I didn't think twice before my lips collided with his in a smooth, relieved kiss. Those strong steady hands grasped my thighs with stability as a groan left his lips. I loved this man. I knew that more than anything else at that moment.

He was my strength and gravity The sound of waves echoed in my ears as the world around us disappeared in a misty haze. I could taste sea salt on his lips as the scent of tequila infiltrated my nose. Our kisses were deep as he explored my mouth with a lazy, languid pace that brought a moan from my throat. I felt him pull back before pressing his forehead against my own.

"Princess," he groaned. "We're supposed to be saving you, not mauling you."

"Can't we do both?" Grover asked with genuine curiosity. I scrambled from Decimus's arms and threw myself into his broad, muscular chest. He chuckled lightly.

"I love you both so much," I whispered. "I should say it way more."

Decimus pressed a soft finger to my lips. "Let's get out of here first. Save the sweet talk for when Kodiak and Blue punish you for leaving the house."

I didn't think through why those words did the exact opposite of scare me.

"How did you find me?" I asked quietly. We slipped down the foyer toward the massive front door. Apparently, my little stalker had shit security.

"Tracker," Grover grinned happily.

We slipped out of the house with silent stealth. I was suddenly delighted that Kodiak was a tad obsessive about my safety. My breathing hitched as I came face to face with a furious Blue. I squeaked out my distress before I was lifted off the ground in a fast movement. Apparently, they had sent the two calmest members of our little family into the building.

"Fucking shit, Vegas," Blue growled sharply. His entire body was trembling, and like a child, I reacted to his emotions. Thick tears began to pour down my face as he pinned me between himself and our large car. My inner turmoil became very apparent then, as I started gasping for air.

Panic attack. I was having a fucking panic attack.

Great timing, Vegas.

"Vegas," Kodiak's voice was so dark. "Who the fuck is in there?"

My response was shaky and nearly pained. "Nathan."

I heard a series of curses and the front door crashing open. I continued to cry into Blue's chest as he asked me a series of quiet questions. So, I told him. I told him about how I followed Nathan back to his place and what he had said. I left out the part about his claims that they had lied to me. I would address that later. I focused on his wild claims about our future and all of the events, outside the bomb, he had claimed. I also expressed my belief that he was not my real stalker and the gaps in his knowledge of my relationship with the boys.

"He's sick, Blue," I mumbled. "Don't hurt him. Please."

Blue snarled against my temple. "Beautiful, I won't hurt him. I'm going to fucking kill him."

I pulled back and gazed into his bright blue eyes. It was undeniable, painfully so, that he meant every bit of his words. Shit. He would kill him. I knew he had killed before. I knew it, but he had never said it. Somehow this was different. I couldn't look away from his intense gaze before nodding. I trusted him. He would do what needed to be done.

My eyes were filled with unnecessary tears, and I found myself curling back into his chest. The entire center of my chest radiated with pain as I struggled to breathe. Blue continued to speak in melodic tones, but my chest pain wouldn't subside. Finally, he pressed a kiss to my forehead and pulled back.

"He's gone, but fuck you should have seen his office," Kodiak declared quietly. It was only then I realized that everyone was surrounding us.

"Later," Blue warned.

"It's really bad, Blue," Bandit mumbled.

I shivered at the sound of his voice as everything inside of me urged me to go to him.

"Is she okay? I mean he didn't..."

Cosimo's words were cut off from a low, dangerous snarl from Kodiak. I looked up at him and shook my head. Blue released my body and offered me up to my big, gruff grizzly bear. In seconds, Kodiak picked me up and nuzzled my throat softly.

"If you think I am ever letting you out of my fucking sight again, you've lost your mind," he whispered tightly against my throat. "I am putting ten more trackers on you."

"Sounds heavy," I sniffed out with a laugh.

"My turn," Booker demanded. He yanked me from Kodiak's unwilling arms and pressed a dozen small kisses along my face and jaw. I began to giggle in earnest as he continued his assault against my tears. Booker always made me smile. He was good at that.

When a sturdy pair of muscled arms wrapped around me from behind I knew Rocket was there. Without a word, he pressed a kiss to the place behind my ear and I let out a sigh of relief. I flushed at the overwhelming intensity of being between the two of them. I placed a kiss on both their cheeks before looking to Cosimo.

"Come here," he motioned. I was released and tumbled into his warm scent. Those crystalline eyes sparkled with unshed tears as he placed a delicate kiss to my lips. Even if he didn't manhandle me, I could feel the intensity and healing power radiating off him in waves.

Finally, I turned around and looked at Bandit. My tears grew heavier as I met his electric green gaze filled with an immense amount of pain. I tossed myself at his chest and brought us both to the soft cold grass. He wrapped his arms around me and I found that I could finally breathe.

"We need to go home," Grover finally mumbled softly. "We don't want to draw attention."

"Plus," Rocket spoke quietly, "we have a stalker to track down."

I nodded and reached for Grover. He easily stood me up and pressed a soft kiss to my forehead before mumbling. "I'm so sorry angel, I promise I'll be better. I should have never left you alone."

I pulled back and grasped his face. "No. This was all him. He's sick, Grover, very, very sick."

Grover shook his head, and those warm brown eyes sparkled with pain. I grasped his shoulders and wrapped my arms around him easily. He moved forward toward the car and let me stay curled up on his lap until Nathan's home lay far behind us.

After a moment, Booker turned from the passenger seat and inspected my face with a level of tension I wasn't used to from him. Blue, from the seat next to Grover, turned to look at me as well.

"Did he cut your hair?" Blue questioned out loud. I could see the idea made him beyond furious. I think Blue would actually kill someone over my hair.

"Um, no," I let out a shaky breath. "That would be me. I decided to get bangs."

The car steeped in silence for a minute before the migration began. Blue tilted his head to the side as Booker nodded with satisfaction. Cosimo brushed my hair gently from behind and whispered something softly in Spanish that sounded like a song. He had always had a beautiful voice. Bandit leaned his head forward and ruffled my hair with satisfaction before letting a grin cover his face.

Kodiak, our driver, spoke. "I think they look great."

Grover echoed those soft sentiments in my ear.

"Decimus, say something, you asshole," Cosimo chuckled. I moved to kneel on Grover's lap and peeked over at my stubborn Greek.

His amber eyes lit up on my face but then narrowed his gaze. "You should have brought one of us with."

I groaned into Grover as he grunted his agreement. Blue chuckled and spoke in a low voice. "We haven't gotten even close to talking about tonight, Beautiful. In fact, we have several things to talk about."

"Like?"

"Why the hell you left? Why you would ever go into Nathan's house or anyone's fucking house without us," Kodiak grunted in a very territorially aggressive way. I didn't need to explain why I had trusted Nathan. He knew damn well. I also detected just a small hint of jealousy and I imagined it looked bad that I had been alone at his house.

I spoke quietly. "I ran into him after my haircut and we were just going to hang out. I shouldn't have gone into his house but I have always trusted him as a friend. You've all been fairly trusting, so I just assumed on some end that I would be safe. So, yeah. But what else do we need to talk about?"

"What we have been keeping from you," Bandit whispered.

"Us," Rocket said confidently.

I didn't respond immediately. I was overwhelmed by a series of emotions. Excitement, frustration, fear, anxiety, and unsurprisingly, lust. I could at least successfully blame the last one on Grover's tight grip on my hips. A grip like that did things to a girl.

My excitement overwhelmed the other emotions. Before I knew it, we had pulled up the driveway of our Victorian home. My eyes trailed across the burnt offering left for me only this morning. Had that been Nathan? I really didn't believe so.

Unfortunately, questions often came with answers. My answer was given to me almost instantaneously. A whimper had worked its way from my throat as I stepped into the foyer. Grover turned to cover my line of sight, but he had been far too late. I had seen it, and I would never, ever, unsee it.

"Oh, wow," I let out a strangled laugh. "Fucking creative."

We were greeted by blood. So much blood that I questioned whether we had painted the foyer without remembering. It dripped from the decorative garland of ravens' heads that hung in full loops and dripped blood onto the smoothly polished flooring. The crimson color of the walls drew attention to our large foyer mirror. How did he get his hands on so many ravens? What about the blood? No fucking way was that from only the birds.

A message awaited us on the mirror.

DON'T LET HIM TAKE CREDIT FOR MY LOVE.

HIS OBSESSION IS NOTHING. HE IS NOTHING.

"Oh, wow," I repeated. My voice sounded rough to me. I could see mirrored expressions from my boys through the reflective surface. Bandit blinked his huge green eyes at me before looking to Kodiak and Blue.

"I think," Blue spoke with darkening eyes, "we should call Edwin."

I wanted to ask. I really did. I just didn't care at this point. I didn't fucking care. Grover's face was pale, and those warm brown eyes seemed to fill with pain. I knew he hated blood. It reminded him of those darker moments of his life. I found my hands wrapping tightly around his waist in comfort. I heard Blue make the call. I even heard Edwin's voice on the other end. What they said, I couldn't tell you. Instead, my gaze was focused on the woman staring back at me through bloody text.

Had I always been this pale? Had my eyes always seemed so dark? So haunted? Grover. He looked very pale. I pressed my forehead against his jaw and felt the cool texture of his chilled skin. Some of the other men had woken from their daze and were talking openly. I couldn't absorb one word of what they were saying.

I wasn't confident how much time had gone by before a loud engine broke my dazed reaction. My eyes fluttered shut for one moment before I stepped back from Grover. He nodded in understanding before moving to stand back.

"Well," Edwin's smooth honey voice drawled. "Lovely decor, little raven."

When I met Edwin's gaze, I found something unexpected. Glee. The fucker was happy to be here. He was delighted he had been called. Why was he here again? Oh, right, I didn't care. I literally had zero room to process his involvement in this bullshit.

I snarled. "Yes. Well. We figured some remodeling was overdue."

His head tilted back in a boisterous laugh before drawing close to me. I couldn't move fast enough to get away from him, to counter his movements. My hands fell back as I caught myself in a pool of warm blood. I felt my hair dip into the puddle as Edwin crawled over me with a satisfied grin.

"Now, now, Vegas. I didn't imagine our first time like this at all. Who knew you were so into blood," he whispered gently. His lethal muscular body spoke only of seduction. From those orange eyes that crackled with crimson flames, to his soft black shoulder-length hair, the man was sin.

"Get off her, Edwin," Kodiak snarled with disgust. I could see his deep green eyes growing darker with anger. Edwin should have been scared. Instead, he laughed.

"Beautiful," he whispered with real enjoyment, "I can practically feel them plotting my death. Aren't loyalty and love a joyous mix? They would do anything for you. I can taste their love. It's palatable. Just like your sweet skin. Your delicious fear."

"You're sick," I growled as my legs and arms began to tremble. I could feel my body begging for release. It wanted to rest on the ground whether it was covered in blood or not. Anything to get away from this demonic man. He pressed forward as my body eased into the pile of blood underneath me.

Why the fuck weren't the boys doing anything?

"They can't," he whispered against my skin. "They can't move or speak."

"What the fuck?" I ignored how the blood squelched under my jeans to peer around his broad back. What I saw? I would never forget it.

I had never believed in the supernatural.

I had never believed in the monsters underneath my bed or in my closet. No. I knew the real monsters were the people we smiled at every single day. It was the woman from the grocery store that beat her husband. It was the old man with a garden shed of dead animals and children.

That said, I couldn't deny the truth of his words.

This was magic.

It had to be why my boys' eyes were clouded in a black cosmic substance. It was beautiful in a demented way. They had no whites to their eyes at all. I blinked to clear the crazy from my line of sight. Instead, the crazy gripped my chin in a vice hold that had me whimpering.

"Let them go," I snarled tightly.

He chuckled again before answering in a dark yet heated tone. "*Dolcezza*, didn't they tell you? Once you enter a deal with the devil, you can never escape."

"You are not a devil," I pushed up, so my chest met his. "You're just a sick freak who is trying to hurt my friends. Is this your idea of a sick joke? The blood? The fire? Has it been you all along?"

I breathed heavily as my body shook with tension. He wanted to jump down the rabbit hole? I would beat him to the fucking bottom. I had lost it officially and never felt more liberated. Was this how Blue felt?

He grinned before licking his lips. "Only a monster can recognize another monster and you Vegas? You are the worst type of monster. You are ruination. It's why I love you."

His words should have garnered a different reaction. Instead, I laughed. My head hit the tile flooring as blood pulsed under me. The worst part? I could still feel our odd connection strumming through me. Surrounding me.

"So, it's been you? This entire time?" Had the ceiling always had blood on it?

He scowled playfully before moving into my line of sight. "Of course not. This is not my style if you catch my drift. It's a little messy. I prefer a quick injection to the vein."

I shook my head.

"See? This is why I like Rocket. You would just burn everything to the ground without the rest of us," he sighed.

Why did he speak as if he knew us? As if he knew me?

"Edwin," another familiar voice called. Byron.

Oh, yes. Because how could this situation get more confusing?

"In here, brother," he sang. Brother? What the hell? You know, I wasn't even surprised anymore. I couldn't be more surprised than I already was. Well, more like horrified, but essentially the same thing.

Byron strode in, tossing the other boys a glance, before kneeling onto our bloodied floor. He wore a bright lilac and green shirt with tan pants. Those poor leather shoes. They would be ruined.

"Have you told her?" he asked, simply. His hand fluttered to my face in a gentle, soothing motion.

"More than they know, but not the same," Edwin sighed with disinterest. Apparently, our game was done for now.

"Explain," my voice strangled. Byron's warm eyes shimmered with power as he raised a hand gently. The blood around me lifted off the floor in a gentle wavering motion. It responded to his pulse that gentle beat inside the skin of his neck. I felt my gaze widen on the trick as he smiled broadly. Then the fucker dropped it. Blood spattered and fell on every part of me.

I looked like Carrie. I was certain to get a disease from this much bird blood on me, right? It couldn't be healthy. Then again. We really had just assumed it was bird blood, we didn't know. We didn't know a damn thing, clearly.

Edwin leaned down to press a light kiss to the corner of my lips. I wish I could tell you that I hadn't responded to it. You know, like a reasonable person? One that wouldn't be attracted to a wild sadistic fucker? When he pulled back, he

193

licked his lips and turned to the other boys. Their empty black eyes turned to a dark gray before resuming their natural color.

Silence filled the foyer.

"Vegas?" Blue looking shocked for the first time in his life.

I fell back onto the tile. "What the hell have you guys gotten us into?"

17

BYRON

*T*he weather had taken a turn. As we sat around the sizeable Victorian living room in silence, thunder shook the house. I had cleaned the foyer easily. Now, we had to make sure our new recruits didn't kill themselves before hearing our rational explanation for the magic we possessed.

Edwin had really made a mess of things.

For instance, his tactics hadn't had his desired response. He had wanted to scare Vegas. Instead, she sat against the couch, covered in blood, while smoking a joint. The other men had expressions that ranged from overwhelmed to furious. Everything and anything in between as well.

My eyes trailed back to Vegas. Beautiful, stunning Vegas. Her long silver hair laid drenched in blood, and that tiny curved body curled against the bottom of the couch. For a blood mage, the entire scene was lust invoking. I was fucked up like that, though.

Those purple eyes stood out in contrast and narrowed on Edwin. I'm sure the guy was getting a hard-on from the way she openly challenged him. Blue sat behind her on the couch and smoothed a large pale hand through her hair in a rhythmic motion. He paid little mind to the blood. I had never seen someone so in tune with their magic before being branded.

Except for Vegas.

"So, magic, huh?" Vegas purred. Her voice was hard and cold. I hated it.

Edwin smiled. "Do you need another demonstration?"

She snarled. "Touch them again, and I'll cut off your balls."

Yep. Total hard on. Fuck. I was sick.

He grinned. "You can do whatever you wish to my balls, sweetheart."

She spat at his feet. He threw his head back and laughed so hard the house shook. I spoke quietly. "How much have you told her?"

Kodiak growled before responding. "Nothing."

It seemed as though everyone else was immobilized. Except for Rocket. He sat on the floor next to Vegas and watched the window with contemplation. Occasionally, his hand pressed to her knee possessively. He didn't seem entirely surprised by this turn of events.

Vegas turned to look at him and then Blue. "You knew about the magic?"

Blue shook his head. "No."

Cosimo, looking oddly calm, responded. "We were contacted by Edwin in May. We were told a private contracting group was interested in hiring us. The mission was exactly what we had been doing anyway. Figure out what was being distributed and by whom."

"So, of course," she drawled, "you didn't tell me."

"We didn't want to bring you into it until we knew they

were for real," Grover grunted. His entire face was pale and shiny. He hated blood. I couldn't understand why. It was beautiful.

She scoffed. "Seems I am brought into it now."

Edwin grinned at that. I had to fight a smile as well because Vegas had very much always been a part of it.

"We had no idea that Byron was involved until recently," Decimus sighed with obvious discomfort. I could see a nicotine patch on his arm. Had he stopped smoking? How unusual for an elemental mage. Vegas handed the joint back to him.

"So," she leaned back with a sigh. "Who the fuck are you? What do you want with my family?"

I smiled at her possessiveness. All five foot something of her tiny body was geared up to kill for them. I had never seen such a fierce woman. She had no concept of self-preservation. Only loyalty and love. If I hadn't had so many years of training under my belt, her raw power would scare the shit out of me.

Edwin smiled. "We want you to join our organization."

"I'm going to need more information than that," she demanded softly, leaning forward.

I moved from my chair and strolled toward a bar cart. I poured myself a drink before responding. "Our organization has morals that align with your own. We are not the good guys. We don't stop just anyone from committing crimes. We are simply contracted out to handle the bad ones on Earth realm. The situations that could affect millions. Lawless justice, I believe you called it. This drug problem on campus? It's small shit compared to what you would be dealing with. However, it is a good experience considering the main suspects are mages as well."

"The Letters?" she spewed.

I sneered. "Unfortunately."

"And you?"

I chuckled. "Undercover. I have been since day one. They don't recognize my family name because we aren't from the American mage circuit. Edwin and I hadn't formed our own team yet within the organization. When I heard about a small gang group handling low-level crimes at the university, I was intrigued. Edwin had already been aware of your presence. Over the past three years, we have been watching and determined that you were worthy of relearning the secret you have all forgotten."

"Which is?"

"Magic, Vegas," Edwin chuckled. "All of you were exposed at a young age and developed the sight. Now, you need to remember what that means."

Vegas paled. "How do you know we have this sight?"

Edwin yanked up the sleeve over his tattoo. I could see her immediately focus on the bright red pattern that looked ready to shimmer off his very skin. I could only imagine the satisfaction that came with being an ink mage.

"Your tattoo?" Bandit asked quietly. His eyes were calm. Still. Out of everyone in their family, Bandit freaked me out the most. He just seemed to be missing...*something.*

"Raise your hand if you know what he is talking about," I whispered. Everyone raised their hand with annoyed expressions. Stupid kids.

"You can only see the tattoo if you have the sight," Edwin trilled.

"Bullshit," Booker swore with venom. He looked annoyed. Flustered even.

"Call your friend, the private investigator," I demanded quietly.

"Is that what she is?" Vegas cursed openly. Her foul mouth only made her hotter. Then she turned on her boys. "Did you know about that as well?"

All of them went quiet. She vibrated with anger. I could see the thread of patience thinning. I needed to finish imparting our information.

"So, my family has lied to me," she snarled. "You two asshats say magic is real. Anything else?"

Edwin stood and walked forward. His hands clasped over her thin shoulders, and his voice leaked out smooth like honey. "I think you know very well, Vegas, that magic is real. I think it doesn't even surprise you. Do you think those flames interacted with anyone else like they did with you? Do you think fire lights up anyone else's soul like yours? I think you knew in your dark little head that something wasn't normal. That you and your family weren't normal."

Vegas began to shake with anger. "Is that why? You want us because we've seen magic, and we're fucked up?"

I spoke loud enough for them to hear. "Remember Carol? She placed all of you together because she knew you had the sight. She's a mage associate."

No one seemed to hear me.

Edwin pulled her close enough to kiss as her head tilted back. "Don't you see Vegas? You are fucked up because you've seen magic. You're trying to live in a world that you know doesn't exist. Others know that you know."

"But we didn't know!" she rose her voice as it finally cracked. "Until you showed up, none of us knew."

Rocket sighed. "Unfortunately, I can't say that with honesty."

"What?" she squeaked.

He nodded with a soft twinkle to his blank face. "Think

about it, Vegas. We have never fit in anywhere. We have always been told that our rough edges make us unlikable. I think it's so much more than that. I think our edges are just fucking fine. We are just made out of a completely different material."

Vegas swayed before her eyes locked on Blue's gaze. "So, this is what? A life-altering decision that we've just made? We believe in magic, our family was placed together because of the fucking sight, and now some assassin organization wants us on their payroll? Are we doing this?"

Ah. She *had* heard me. Good.

Blue hummed before smiling brightly. "I guess so, beautiful."

Decimus chuckled darkly. "This is so fucked."

Our little starlight froze on the spot and moved her gaze to mine. I could see those indigo eyes shattering to release a manic inner light. Good. We liked them crazy. Humans had such a limited mindset.

"If you hurt my family, I will be your ruin," she hissed tightly before turning toward the doors. Her bare, bloody feet trailed deep red footprints.

She would be our ruin either way.

"Don't you want to know the name of our group?" Edwin asked quietly. Thunder moved through the house like an earthquake.

"Why the fuck not!" She laughed with furious eyes. I wanted to tell her. I wanted to warn her. She needed to speak softer. The monster in my blood loved her panic.

Edwin leaned back into his chair. "The Red Masques, little raven. We are, you are now part of the Red Masques."

I closed my eyes as contentment filled me. That name. Our new team. Our new family. Our new life.

I barely noticed the living room door slam shut.

VEGAS

I knew one thing. Only one thing. I loved those boys.

They owned my soul. They held every part of me.

If it took becoming part of this bullshit to keep them safe, I would. I would sign my soul to Edwin if it meant keeping them safe. Life without them wasn't a life. My bathroom mirror clouded with fog from the shower. I ran through my thoughts trying to process my feelings toward this peculiar situation. First, we were fucked up because we had seen magic before. Now we were living a half-life but could gain back some sanity...with magic? I supposed that was their fix to our problem. Second, we had been placed together from a young age. What about Lucida though? Did she not have sight? What fucking part did she play in all this? If I had to assume, she most likely knew about the new contract but clearly not the magic aspect. That hurt. It hurt that she didn't tell me. Third, I had been lied to. Magic existed. The boys had tried to keep me safe but shielded us from a much more horrifying reality. We had been exposed. We didn't have a choice now. We had to join. Someone, most likely, my bloody stalker now was aware of our knowledge.

My head hit the tile of the shower. Water streamed down my skin and created a pink waterfall that cascaded down the drain. Oddly, I didn't feel anxious. I only felt overwhelmed. That was reasonable. My guess? The crack in my sanity was here to stay. I did the only thing I could do and wash my entire body free of the blood from downstairs.

"Vegas?"

"Grover?" I called out. He entered and didn't bat a lash at

my naked body. I stood in the shower and met his gaze. Both of us were running on empty.

"Angel," he whispered through a pained expression. I turned off the shower and stepped toward him. My hands fluttered to his cheekbones where I placed two soft kisses.

"This is real, isn't it?"

Grover's hands grasped my waist as he lifted me level with his own gaze. I wrapped my legs around him as he nuzzled my throat gently. My slight whimper echoed through the room as he looked into my wide-eyed expression.

"Down there was real. What they said was real. So real," he whispered with a horrified expression. "And this. You and me. This is real."

My hands found his hair as he pressed into me. Our lips connected in a fusion of warmth. I groaned into his sweet hot kiss that reminded me of chilly fireplace lit evenings. Grover's hands tightened on my thighs in a bruising grip that made my skin prickle in anticipation. My naked heat pressed against his belt buckle as he angled me on the counter so that I leaned back. His gaze was molten lava as he inspected every inch of my naked form with a very possessive expression.

"Grover," I moaned into his mouth. Those long rough fingers pet my heat with gentle, careful touches. He touched me like I was an irreplaceable treasure.

"God, Vegas," he bit my neck gently. "You are so wet, angel."

I felt my hips move against his fingers as he nibbled down my throat and chest gently. He didn't bruise, he didn't bite. No, he kept up his slow torture as my pleasure rose in thick, consuming waves. I could feel every ounce of tension and insanity rise to a toxic mixture under my skin. My pleasure nearly felt painful.

"Come for me," he demanded in soft, husky undertones. I moaned into his mouth as my heat surrounded him and refused to let go. His fingers continued their precise movements until I gasped out his name. A cold sweat broke over my skin as he rewarded me with soft kisses to my flushed face.

"Shit," I whispered against his lips.

"No, little raven," Edwin spoke from the door. "That was hot. Not shit."

I groaned as Grover let out a deep feral growl. Edwin chuckled but tossed me a towel with an agility no one should possess.

"What the fuck do you want?" I snarled.

"We are going out," he smirked with a heated gaze. "Get some damned clothes on. You're asking for someone to fuck you."

I rolled my eyes. "As long as it's not you."

Grover chuckled softly.

The air stilled as Edwin's lips tugged on my ear and sent a thrill through me. "You're lucky I like consent, little girl."

I turned to smack his stupid face. He was gone though, and Grover seemed shaken by his speed. It was unnatural. Obviously. He was a mage. Whatever that was. I kissed Grover softly before he strode out. I saw a bit of his usual swagger peeking out and let my thighs brush together as a reminder of his touch. My image in the mirror seemed far more revitalized than before. The blood had been washed out of my long hair so I swept it into an easy braid. I shimmied on a pair of skinny black jeans and an oversized hoodie. It smelled like Bandit. Once I had slid on sneakers, I made my way to the staircase. The foyer looked untouched now. Byron had said he was a blood mage, right?

"She isn't going," the familiar protective tone made me smile. It seemed the boys were faring well.

"She is," Edwin chided. "She is as much a part of this team as any of you."

All right. That earned him some brownie points. Well, maybe brownie crumbs.

"I have questions," I muttered.

"Can they wait?" Byron shot back, "I know it's a lot to ask you to blindly agree."

Could they? I guess I could wait. I had a feeling this thing he wanted to do was important. Plus, I wasn't even sure where to start. Who were the Red Masques? I looked around the room. Except for Blue, my boys were watching my expressions and reactions. I offered an annoyed grimace.

"If," I exhaled softly, "we join your group. Will we be able to stay together, as a family?"

Edwin chuckled. "Sure, you will just earn two new members."

Byron nodded his consent. How could they be brothers?

I locked eyes with Blue. I could see he wanted to do this. My gaze fell to Kodiak. His complexion was flushed and annoyed, but he didn't seem scared. Neither did Decimus. No, he actually looked bored. Asshole.

Rocket and Booker whispered but kept their gaze on me. Both of them gave subtle nods. I felt a hand slid into mine and found Cosimo there. He kissed my cheek as Bandit's long arms slipped around my waist gently. Finally, I found Grover's form lounged against the wall. His dark twinkling eyes highlighted his smile.

Shit. They were in. I could even go as far as to say that they wanted this.

I looked at Byron, ignoring Edwin, and offered a sharp nod. "Fine. We're in. But we are going to need way more information after tonight."

Edwin answered before Byron could. "Don't you worry, Vegas. We are an open book for your pleasure. After all, we are family, now."

My chest locked in annoyance. This was going to be a fucked up relationship.

18

VEGAS

*E*dwin's plan left me cold. Literally. I froze my tits off. I pressed my back into the alley wall for some relief from the wind. When had winter arrived?

"Don't worry, Vegas," Byron assured softly with a shoulder squeeze. "This will be over soon."

"Touch her again, and you die," Blue snarled from my other side. I grinned at his possessive tone. Byron scoffed but kept his eyes trained on the empty alley. We had been here for nearly an hour.

A door opened. The rusted joints screamed in protest. A chorus of deep chuckles echoed through the small space. I focused on the low grunt I heard instead.

"You stupid fuck," a familiar voice growled.

K.

Another voice spoke in smooth low tones. "Get the fuck off me."

"Alexander's little baby brother," A cooed. Everyone laughed louder.

"He wanted to join us so bad he would have done anything," K chuckled. I could see him gripping his junk as he snarled in Levi's red face. I shuddered at the sight of him pressed against the brick wall by A's elbow.

"Well, he's dead now," Levi said with no emotion. "Does it really fucking matter?"

K smiled. "Yeah, it fucking matters, Levi. The girl didn't die. Your brother couldn't even manage to get that right. We can't go after them without starting trouble so we needed his dumb fucking ass."

"Shut the fuck up about him," Levi growled.

"Is that why you tried to blow our shit to pieces?" A laughed. "You think a bomb would kill us? No. Not so easy, little Levi."

"You stupid fucks deserve to die," he muttered through a rasp. "He wanted to join your stupid group so bad he went and got himself killed."

Ah, that answered several questions. Levi had planted the bomb, but his brother was the one who had tried to kill me. Now, Alexander, as they said, was dead. Peachy.

I can't imagine *who* would have killed him. Shit. Why wasn't I more upset?

"He shouldn't have missed that shot then," K grinned.

"They would have killed him either way!" Levi screamed through tears. Oh, fuck.

"Yes," A sighed. "That much is true."

"Is that what you're going to do to me? Kill me?" Levi chuckled then. It was a sick, low sound that had my soul breaking. I could taste his depression and hopelessness from here.

"Without a doubt," K muttered. "We do need to ask you a few questions first."

"Where the fuck is B?" A growled. Someone muttered an answer. It was only then that I realized B had slipped away. His appearance through the back alley door was startling. It caused my stomach to churn.

"Levi," B chuckled a coarse laugh. "I would say good to see you, but it won't be. For you at least."

I had a sick feeling about this. My eyes tracked a shadow from across the way. Edwin's vibrant orange eyes blinked at me. He flashed me a wicked smile before pressing a silencing finger to his lips. I rolled my eyes. Blue's arm snagged my waist possessively. It only made Edwin's grin grow. He was an odd man.

"Okay," B sighed. "First question, Levi."

I watched as B's hand lit up red and moved down the soft flesh at Levi's throat. I saw a sick, pale sheen claim Levi's face at contact.

"How much did Alexander tell you?" K snarled.

"About?" Levi gasped.

"Our business," K kept it simple.

"Why would he know about that?" B shot him a confused look. "You don't even tell us that shit."

K snarled. "Shut it, blood boy."

I saw B roll his eyes as he tightened his grip. My eyes tracked Levi's faint pulse and trembling body. K stepped forward. "Now, exactly what did Alexander tell you?"

Levi chuckled. "He didn't tell me shit."

"Bullshit," A growled. "We know he was in the attic." A stunned hush came over the group. Levi sighed with a strangled voice.

"Whatever he saw," Levi licked his dry lips, "he kept to himself."

Then A lost it. I mean really lost it. B's eyes widen as A began pounding into Levi with uncontrolled rage. My feet moved forward as Blue locked me into place. I barely restrained my fury. I hated bullies.

"You're going to kill him," K sighed.

"I have something that may work," B offered with an indifferent expression. He didn't wholly fool me though. No, there was a tightness to his jaw and eyes. He didn't like this. It didn't bring him pleasure hurting someone that had clearly gotten mixed up in the wrong shit.

Wait. He had blown up the student pavilion.

Yep. Sympathy evaporated.

"What's that, blood boy?"

"I stole a new batch of truth from my bro," he sighed.

K clapped. "Wonderful."

A groaned but shook off his wrists. "Do it before I kill him."

B moved toward Levi with the prepped syringe but looked up at K first. "Lend me a hand boss? He won't be able to talk very loud after your guard dog tore at his throat."

I could have told you B's plan in retrospect. It didn't stop my eyes going wide in shock. The minute K knelt down, the plan exploded, and several events occurred simultaneously.

B moved unusually fast to inject the syringe into K's scrawny neck. A guttural growl came from A as he lunged forward. Edwin was far quicker though. His muscular tall body smashed into A's and caused the huge man to collapse. I saw a glint of silver followed by red before my boys surrounded the other Letters. Blue let out an amused chuckle against my ear.

"You like this?" I whispered. It wasn't in a disappointed way either. I was curious.

Blue hummed while pressing a kiss to my neck. "Hell, yes. Those fuckers deserved this."

B stood with agility and spread his hands out with cocky ease. He tucked a recording device into his pocket before his hands began to glow red. With a predatorial grace, he stalked toward each Letter. I wish I could have said he knocked them unconscious.

No. He killed them.

Magic. A complex subject that I didn't understand. However, I did realize that one equaled one. The equation with Byron? Magic glowing hands equaled blood pouring out of every exit of his victim's body. By the end of his session, he grinned and clapped his hands once in satisfaction.

Obviously, sanity wasn't a family trait. Edwin smiled at me.

Aw, crap. I had voiced my opinion out loud.

"Li'l raven," he grinned. "We all have our own brand of crazy. Now, that we have recorded proof of their product lacing, we can destroy it with yours."

"What did they lace it with?" Blue voiced.

"Ink magic," Edwin spoke in a more serious tone. "Intense high, amazing trip, and highly poisonous."

"Ah," Rocket nodded. "Explains why I didn't recognize the chemical composition."

"So," I breathed out my excitement, "when you say my brand of crazy..."

I had a good feeling about his next words. I figured if magic was real, maybe my pyromaniac tendencies could be excused. I had already fallen down the rabbit hole... nowhere to go but down, right?

Edwin's eyes sparkled with light before he tossed an object my way. I felt Blue's arms wrap around my waist in a constrictive hug. I examined the lighter in my hand before turning back to the pile of bodies being doused in gasoline. Fire covered most crimes.

"I wasn't going to include that," Edwin drawled. "but if you want to."

Grover grasped my face with concerned eyes. "You don't have to angel."

Those brown eyes were filled with fear. Fear for me. I pressed my lips to him in a soft silky kiss. I whispered softly against his ear. "I want to Grover. It's different than before. They seemed like real jerks, now they are dead. What's the harm in lighting them on fire?"

Decimus grinned a crooked smile. "Yu speak crazy, and I get turned on. That's fucked up. Right?"

Booker grinned. "Nah, she could drink coffee, and I'd spring a hard-on."

I laughed at that. Grover continued to shadow me. I noticed Kodiak stood next to me as well. I knelt down gently before flicking my finger over the creative fire breathing device. Within seconds, my flame had turned into a firestorm. The smell of flesh burning crisped the air. I laughed softly as Kodiak threw me over his shoulder and stalked toward our waiting cars.

"Bandit," I whispered softly. He kissed my lips softly as Kodiak let out a warning growl. I ruffled the grizzly bear's hair and nuzzled his neck softly. He was very stressed right now.

"Where next?" Rocket asked quietly. I noticed that over his shoulder was a bloody and unconscious Levi. Shit, I hadn't even checked for him before setting the pile on fire. I'm a terrible coffee date.

"The Letters' house. We have a stash to burn," Byron explained. I noticed his walk had a bounce. I wondered how using magic affected him.

"More burning?" I voiced out loud.

Everyone chuckled, except Grover, as Cosimo voiced my own concern., "*Mierda*, we've officially lost it, right?"

Byron's smooth voice echoed around us, "No. You've lost nothing, you're just starting your journey."

Edwin chuckled. "Now, little raven, let's go burn their shit."

EDWIN

I hadn't lied. She was a monster.

A sweet toxic monster that had claws sharp enough to rival any predator. In time she would turn into my ruination. I had no doubt. It doubled my attraction for her.

"She shouldn't do this," Grover muttered. My senses heightened to draw on the energies around me. I needed to know who held any misconceptions about her abilities. That would need to be handled now.

"One thing you will need to understand, Ravens," I exhaled.

We stood in front of The Letters' large mansion. The lights were off, and the gasoline was set. Our silver-haired Raven stood confidently in front of us all. I could see her fiddling with the lighter as she considered her actions, for just a moment. Then she lit the flame and held it level with the set lighter fluid trail.

I watched as a stunning smile broke onto her angular features. The flames reflected against her creamy skin and silky hair like it had been born to do so. It had. Those soft lips pressed together in anticipation. The fire moved closer to the house as she stepped forward to follow.

Blue captured her waist but it didn't stop his lips from splitting into a grin. Decimus stood near him with a thoughtful expression in his dark eyes. The unconscious body, Levi, laid over Rocket's shoulder. The stoic doctor switched his indifferent gaze between the starry sky and Vegas. I understood. She drew my attention easy as well.

I continued. "Everyone here has darkness. Even *her*. Especially her," I explained quietly to Grover. His eyes sparked with his own darkness as Kodiak let out a nearby grunt.

"Why her?" Bandit asked quietly.

"Why us?" Cosimo added.

"Once you understand more about us, you will understand your place in our group," Byron explained. "As for her?"

I spoke up. "Have you ever seen someone so selfless? Someone with so little sense of self-preservation? The only thing she lives for is her family. That type of loyalty and love is absolutely unique. It isn't human nature to act as she does."

"We won't let you exploit her," Booker commented calmly. Rocket looked back with a nod. He really had terrific hearing.

"Exploit her?" I drawled. "No, boys, you misunderstand. She is the key to this team, the center, the battery."

"What?" Grover asked with a frown.

"Vegas is a tad different from you eight sight holders," I watched her. "She didn't just see magic...*she is magic*."

EPILOGUE

*T*he room blazed with fire. In the center of the room stood a massive stone altar that a boy with orange eyes watched with captivation. His mentor, Nicholas, stilled his anxious movements with a large hand upon his shoulder.

"You're positive this will work?" A large man in black leather inquired.

Nicholas nodded before stepping toward the altar. Ten rings of fire surrounded the altar in a circular pattern. They flickered with an unnatural silver and blue light. The boy was careful to match the path of his mentor until they reached the calm center.

A woman with large blue eyes stood next to the altar. She trembled in the presence of the boy's mentor. Most did. The boy watched with fascination as his mentor crafted the woman's will.

The Queen's intention is our will.

His mentor said that often. The flames grew hotter and jumped onto the altar with enthusiasm. They wanted to do this. They craved this creation.

When the air popped with tension and the ten rings of flames settled, a small cry echoed out in the night. A child had been made. The boy with orange eyes moved to stand near his mentor and peered at the altar. A child had been made. A child with silver hair and indigo eyes. A child of fire.

M. SINCLAIR

INTERNATIONAL & US BEST SELLER

M. Sinclair is a Chicago native, parent to 3 cats, and can be found writing almost every moment of the day. Despite being new to publishing, M. Sinclair has been writing for nearly 10 years now. Currently, in love with the Reverse Harem genre, she plans to publish an array of works that are considered romance, suspense, and horror within the year. M. Sinclair lives by the notion that there is enough room for all types of heroines in this world and being saved is as important as saving others. If you love fantasy romance, obsessive possessive alpha males, and tough FMCs, then M. Sinclair is for you!

Just remember to love cats... that's not negotiable.

ALSO BY M. SINCLAIR

Vengeance Series

#graysguards

Book 1 - Savages

Book 2 - Lunatics

Book 3 - Monsters

Book 4 - Psychos

Complete Series

The Red Masques Series

#vegasandherboys

Book 1 - Raven Blood

Book 2 - Ashes & Bones

Book 3 - Shadow Glass

Book 4 - Fire & Smoke

Book 5 - Dark King

Complete Series

Tears of the Siren Series

#lorcanslovers

Book 1 - Horror of Your Heart

Book 2 - Broken House

Book 3 - *Announced soon!*

The Dead and Not So Dead Trilogy

#narcshotties

Book 1 - Queen of the Dead

Book 2 - Tea Time with the Dead

Book 3 - *Announced soon!*

Descendant Series

#novasmages

Book 1 - Descendant of Chaos

Book 2 - Descendant of Blood

Book 3 - Descendant of Sin (*coming soon!*)

Reborn Series

#mayasmages

Book 1 - Reborn In Flames

Book 2 - Soaring in Flames

The Wronged Trilogy

#valentinasvigilanties

Book 1 - Wicked Blaze Correctional

Standalones

Peridot (Jewels Cafe Series)

Collaborations

Rebel Hearts Heists Duet *(M. Sinclair & Melissa Adams)*

Book 1 - Steal Me

Forbidden Fairytales *(The Grim Sisters - M. Sinclair & CY Jones)*

Book 1 - Stolen Hood

Book 2 - Knights of Sin

Book 3 - Deadly Games

Join our Group on Facebook The Grim Sisters Reading Group.

STALK ME... REALLY, I'M INTO IT

Instagram: msinclairwrites
Facebook: Sinclair's Ravens (New content announced!)
Twitter: @writes_sinclair

Printed in Great Britain
by Amazon

43908369R00131